"He's got a gu[...]man shrieked in terror. [...]

Her scream crea[...][...]sperately tried to remove the young woman from between himself and the murder suspect, a single shot filled the railroad car. Longarm felt a slug sear his right shoulder. The blonde in his arms cried out and Longarm spun her aside and tried to raise his weapon but his arm wasn't responding to his command.

The big man was on his feet and in the aisle now. "Marshal, drop your gun or I'll kill you and anyone else who tries to interfere!"

The matronly woman's hysterical screams grew even louder and more shrill.

"Woman," the killer raged, "shut your yap!"

When the older woman didn't obey his command, the big man shot her in the chest. A scream died on her lips and she tumbled back into the seat, eyelids fluttering a moment before she died.

Longarm was enraged. "Dammit, you didn't have to kill her!"

"Don't move, Marshal, or your name is on my next bullet."

DON'T MISS THESE
ALL-ACTION WESTERN SERIES
FROM THE BERKLEY PUBLISHING GROUP

THE GUNSMITH by J. R. Roberts
Clint Adams was a legend among lawmen, outlaws, and ladies. They called him . . . the Gunsmith.

LONGARM by Tabor Evans
The popular long-running series about Deputy U.S. Marshal Long—his life, his loves, his fight for justice.

SLOCUM by Jake Logan
Today's longest-running action Western. John Slocum rides a deadly trail of hot blood and cold steel.

BUSHWHACKERS by B. J. Lanagan
An action-packed series by the creators of Longarm! The rousing adventures of the most brutal gang of cutthroats ever assembled—Quantrill's Raiders.

DIAMONDBACK by Guy Brewer
Dex Yancey is Diamondback, a Southern gentleman turned con man when his brother cheats him out of the family fortune. Ladies love him. Gamblers hate him. But nobody pulls one over on Dex. . . .

WILDGUN by Jack Hanson
The blazing adventures of mountain man Will Barlow—from the creators of Longarm!

TEXAS TRACKER by Tom Calhoun
Meet J. T. Law: the most relentless—and dangerous— manhunter in all Texas. Where sheriffs and posses fail, he's the best man to bring in the most vicious outlaws—for a price.

W   C-1

TABOR EVANS

LONGARM

AND THE
MONTANA MADMEN

JOVE BOOKS, NEW YORK

This is a work of fiction. Names, characters, places, and incidents either are the product of the author's imagination or are used fictitiously, and any resemblance to actual persons living or dead, business establishments, events, or locales is entirely coincidental.

LONGARM AND THE MONTANA MADMEN

A Jove Book / published by arrangement with the author

PRINTING HISTORY
Jove edition / July 2004

ISBN: 0-515-13774-X

A JOVE BOOK®
Jove Books are published by The Berkley Publishing Group, a division of Penguin Group (USA) Inc., 375 Hudson Street, New York, New York 10014. JOVE and the "J" design are trademarks belonging to Penguin Group (USA) Inc.

PRINTED IN THE UNITED STATES OF AMERICA

10 9 8 7 6 5 4 3 2 1

Chapter 1

It had been warmish for mid-October when Deputy United States Marshal Custis Long exited his Denver federal office building and saw the brutal crime being committed. There were two men, big and bearded, who had overtaken a lone pedestrian walking along Colfax Avenue. As they came abreast of their victim, the men each pressed revolvers into the victim's side. Longarm might not even have noticed the crime if the victim had not objected and tried to fight off his assailants. Had the victim been smart, he simply would have handed over his wallet, but that was not the case and he was shot in both sides of the body.

The gunshots were muffled but distinct. Longarm saw the two thugs grab the man, support his sagging body while they expertly lifted his money and jewelry, then carry him to a street bench and deposit him there with his head down on his chest and his blood leaking from his gunshot wounds.

"Hey!" Longarm shouted, from half a block away as

he drew his gun knowing he could not risk shooting and wounding an innocent bystander. "Stop!"

But the two assailants had no intention of stopping. Instead, they took off running down the crowded downtown street. They were smart enough to split up and each head up a different side street. When Longarm reached the victim, the wounded man was alive . . . but just barely. There was an older woman with a pink parasol standing in front of him screaming in abject horror.

"Find a doctor!" Longarm commanded, but the lady was too shocked to do anything but continue screaming. Other pedestrians seemed confused and helpless so Longarm tore off the victim's ruined coat and then his shirt to try to staunch the bleeding.

"Am I dying?" the man whispered.

"I don't know but you're losing a great deal of blood. I'm going to have you lie down on this bench and then I'm going to try and stop the bleeding. Do you know those men that robbed and shot you?"

"No," the victim whispered, his face pale and his eyes wide with fright. "Are you a doctor?"

"Afraid not. I'm a federal law officer. But I've seen a lot of gunshot wounds and, I'm sorry to say, you're in bad shape."

The man raised a shaky hand. "I don't want to die! I'm only thirty-three years old and I've got a wife and family!"

"What's your name and where do you live?"

"My name is Chester King. I live in . . ."

A sudden convulsion racked the man's entire body and he tried but failed to continue speaking. Longarm had seen a lot of gunshot victims and he didn't think this one had any chance of survival.

"Just take it easy, Mr. King. I'm going to try and stop this bleeding and I'm sure that a doctor will be here soon." Longarm twisted around and angrily shouted, "Woman, stop that infernal screaming and find me a doctor!"

His tongue-lashing sent the woman reeling backward and then she turned and hurried up the street.

"Damn," Longarm choked in rage. "Someone . . . anyone . . . get a doctor!"

Longarm was hoping that the two bullets might have ricocheted off the victim's ribs or at least passed completely through his body. As he gently turned the man on his side, he could see that one bullet had exited but that the other was still inside.

"I'm a doctor," a small man with a red handlebar mustache and a medical bag said, appearing from the gawking crowd. "Stand aside."

Longarm moved back and hovered over the doctor's shoulder hoping that the doctor was a miracle worker. He watched as the physician worked frantically to stem the bleeding with bandages he tore from his black leather bag. After less than a minute, Longarm saw that he was successful in stopping the hemorrhaging.

"Who are you?" the doctor demanded, not looking up.

"I'm a federal officer of the law."

"We need to get this man to the Denver Hospital immediately. Can you commandeer a vehicle?"

"You bet I can," Longarm assured the physician.

He ran out into the street, looked up and down the line of carriages, buckboards, freight wagons and coaches, then ran to a buckboard and ordered its driver to pull over near the gunshot victim.

"But I've got supplies to pick up at the feed store," the driver protested.

3

"Do what I say!" Longarm shouted, showing the reluctant driver his badge and then grabbing one of his horses by the bit. "Turn your wagon this way and help us get this wounded man to the hospital."

But the driver didn't give a damn about being helpful or even a Good Samaritan. Instead, he tried to rein his team off Longarm who then released his grip on the horse's bit and jumped up beside the driver.

"Hey!" the man protested.

Longarm was so disgusted by the driver's attitude that he drew back his fist and slammed it into the driver's face, knocking him completely over the seat to land unconscious in the bed of his wagon. A moment later, Longarm was helping the doctor load the unconscious victim into the back of the buckboard and then he drove the wagon hard up the street toward the hospital.

"Doc, has King got a chance?"

"If he didn't," the physician yelled, "we wouldn't be risking our lives racing up Colfax in all this traffic. Marshal, watch your driving. You almost ran over a woman and her child!"

It seemed to take forever to reach the hospital. When they arrived, Longarm set the wagon's brake then raced in the front door and summoned the staff to run out with him to the wagon.

"He's still alive," the doctor said to the hospital staff.

One of the attendants asked, "Which surgery room do you want him to be taken to, Dr. Randall?"

"Number two. Easy with him now! I'll be right along."

Longarm was standing beside the buckboard and now he grabbed the physician by the sleeve and told him the victim's name adding, "I think the man is from out of town, but he fainted before I could find out anything more."

"I'm sure he has some identification on his person."

"No," Longarm said. "The two big fellas that shot him on the street took his wallet. If King dies, we'll have a devil of a time determining who he is and where he lived."

"Well," the doctor said, starting to leave, "that's not my problem. But I think the man has a chance if we can extract the bullet and no vital organs were pierced. Your job is to catch the muggers that shot him and see that they are brought to justice."

"Right," Longarm said, watching Dr. Randall bound up the front steps of the hospital and disappear through the open doors.

Longarm stuck around the hospital until nine o'clock that night hoping that Dr. Randall would appear from surgery and tell him that King was going to survive. But the doctor never appeared and, finally, Longarm headed back to his apartment determined to return to the hospital the next day and find out what he could about King regardless of whether the man had lived or died.

Longarm had been a law officer for many years but the savagery of this shooting got to him deep in the gut, and so later that evening he went to the Blue Heron Saloon for a couple of rye whiskies. The bartender, an old friend named Norman, noticed Longarm seemed subdued.

"What's the matter, Custis? You look lower than a snake's belly."

Longarm told Norman about how King had been gunned down in the middle of Colfax Street with hundreds of people watching. "They just ran up on either side of this guy and opened fire at point-blank range. I don't know how in the world he's still alive. The doc says he has a fighting chance, but I think he's being optimistic."

Norman shrugged. "Some guys fall over dead if they get a needle prick on the finger and others . . . well, I've seen a few gunfights right here in this saloon where men were shot to pieces and somehow survived. This King guy might be one of those that refuse to cash in his chips."

"I hope you're right," Longarm said, sipping his rye. "But he lost so much blood that he was white and turning gray."

"That's a bad sign."

"Real bad," Longarm agreed. "Norman, have you ever been shot?"

"Oh sure," the bartender said, grinning broadly. "I got a bullet in my butt! It's so deep the doc said I'd be better off being a *lead* ass than a *dead* ass."

"Get out of here," Longarm said with a smile.

"Say," Norman said, "I'll bet you've been shot a few times."

"More than I care to remember. Also, I've been stabbed, clubbed and poisoned."

"Poisoned?"

"Yep," Longarm assured the man. "By a woman in Reno. She and I were up in her hotel room having some fun and she spiked my drink with arsenic."

Norman noticed Longarm's drink was low so he topped it off. "Arsenic is supposed to always be fatal."

"That's what they say," Longarm answered. "But in my case, it just gave me a severe case of the scoots."

"Did you arrest the woman that tried to do you in?"

"I did," Longarm replied, "but she was such a popular saloon girl that I doubt she served much time in jail. She just claimed that someone else must have poisoned me before I got up to her room. It would have been impossible to prove she was lying and I had to leave town. But I tell you this, I'll never get near her again!"

"So why do you think this King fella was robbed and shot in broad daylight?" Norman asked. "I mean, why would anyone be so bold and take that kind of risk?"

"I've been asking myself the same question."

"Did you get a good look at them?"

Longarm took another sip of his drink. "I wouldn't say it was a good look, but I believe I'd recognize the pair, if I saw them together on the street. They were both huge men and not at all the kind you'd want to meet in a dark alley."

Norman shook his head. "The sad truth of the matter is that this town is going to the dogs. It's getting so even a man has to be careful where he goes or else he'll get mugged . . . or worse."

Longarm nodded in agreement. Denver was becoming a mecca for gamblers, prostitutes, hustlers and criminals. Every day there was at least one killing, although many of them were caused by domestic disputes.

He finished his drink and paid his bill. "I think I'll go back to the hospital just in case there's some news."

"You're a *federal* law officer," Norman reminded him. "Why don't you just leave it to the local authorities?"

"Can't do that," Longarm said. "When you've seen a man shot before your eyes and tried to save his life, you get involved. It's hard to explain, but that's just the way I feel."

"And it's why you're a good man and officer," Norman said. "I hope that your friend survives."

"He's not my friend, but I hope you're right," Longarm called over his shoulder as he headed out the door.

• • •

When he arrived back at the Denver Hospital, Longarm was informed by an orderly that Dr. Randall had gone home for the night.

"What about his patient, Mr. King?"

"Oh, he died. He's laid out in the basement probably already stiff as a board."

Longarm should not have cared that much, but the cold way that he was told was galling. Not bothering to curb his anger, he snapped, "Just like you and I will be some day."

The orderly's eyes widened and then he gulped. "I guess you're right. But I don't want to die all shot up in the street with people watching. When I cash in, I want it to be in bed humping some young woman under twenty."

Longarm had no use for this man so he showed his badge and said, "I'd like to see King and inspect whatever belongings were on his person."

"He was robbed."

"He had a ring and jewelry and probably other things besides his wallet when he was mugged. Where are his clothes?"

"In the trash, but they are all bloody."

"I'll have a look at them first."

The orderly had been about to consume a sandwich wrapped in brown paper. It smelled like a sardine sandwich, which Longarm thought very unappetizing. Clearly not happy with this delay, the orderly said, "I sure don't see why you want to see his clothes, but that's your business."

"Exactly."

The orderly shrugged, trying to act as if he didn't care

8

one way or the other. He was a pale and skinny fellow in his thirties with a few wispy chin whiskers, close set eyes and not much of a chin. Longarm thought he was probably even dumber than he appeared.

"The trash is in back," the man said. "I ain't goin' through it. There's some awful stuff in hospital trash. A man could get gangrene or diseased by touching it, but if you want to take that foolish chance, it's your call, Marshal."

Longarm could barely stomach this imbecile so he said nothing but followed the man down hallways and past closed surgery and patient rooms until they finally entered a large storage area that had the stench of carbolic acid, antiseptics and other things that he cared not to consider.

"The trash cans are over there by the wall."

"Which one should I look in?"

"Beats me."

Longarm walked over to the row of trash cans and inspected them without touch. He knew that he would recognize King's coat, shirt and pants, and he did after only a few minutes because he got lucky and they were on top of a heap.

The orderly wanted to leave. "You don't need me here, do you?"

"No. Go eat your damned sardines."

"Foolishness," the man muttered just loud enough for Longarm to hear as he scuttled out the door.

Longarm wasn't thrilled with examining the dead man's clothing, but he knew that King had been well-tailored and that meant that there might be tags indicating where his clothing was made. Sure enough, he discovered this to be the case. Right on the inside pocket of the jacket, still damp with blood, was a tailor's tag that read:

William Benton Fine Apparel, Helena, MT.

"That's interesting," Longarm mused aloud as he gingerly pulled out the pockets hoping that something might have been missed. But he found nothing of interest and soon was back bothering the orderly whose cheeks were stuffed with bread and fish.

"I want to see his personal items. Watch. Ring."

"Maybe he didn't have none."

"He did," Longarm countered. "Where are they?"

The orderly had to swallow hard. "They lock up all that stuff. You can't get it until tomorrow 'cause they don't give me the combination to the safe."

"For good reason I'm sure," Longarm told the man as he went back out the door and into the street.

He would return in the morning and inspect King's belongings. Then, he would fire off a telegram to Helena, Montana and ask that a notice be placed in the town's newspaper instructing any relatives of the deceased that Chester King was dead and that his personal belongings could be sent for . . . if someone didn't steal them first. That happened quite often, and it was just another sign of the times in Denver.

But at the very least, Longarm would be able to let an anxious wife or children, parents or friends know that the innocent man they had loved had been callously murdered in broad daylight on the streets of Denver.

Chapter 2

It was ten o'clock in the morning when Longarm returned from the hospital and arrived at his office. His boss, Marshal Billy Vail, stepped up to Longarm's desk and said, "You have another rough night?"

Longarm looked up at the smaller man who was his friend. "What is that supposed to mean?"

"The morning is half over."

"Yeah," Longarm admitted, "it is. Sit down, Billy. I have something to show you."

Longarm opened a small leather pouch that he had gotten from the Denver Hospital's safe. He poured the contents of the pouch on his desk and said, "I was witness to a man who was gunned down about two blocks from this building yesterday afternoon. It was a savage execution by two men who got away clean."

"Why didn't you pursue them?"

"I'd hoped the man they'd shot might have a chance to live so I stayed with him all the way to the hospital. His name was Chester King and, from the tag on his coat, I suspect that he lived in Helena, Montana."

11

Billy stared at the deceased's simple gold wedding band and a rather expensive pocket watch. "I guess they didn't have time to get everything."

"No," Longarm said, "they didn't."

"How unfortunate that Mr. King died. That's exactly the kind of thing that gives Denver a mean reputation. I assume that the local authorities have interviewed you and are trying to solve the murder."

"I haven't spoken to them yet," Longarm admitted.

Billy's eyebrows raised in question. "Custis, you must do so at once."

Longarm placed his hand on the gold watch. "I was going to until I saw this," he said, turning the watch over so that Billy could read the following inscription: TO UNITED STATES MARSHAL JED KING FOR HIS COURAGEOUS YEARS OF SERVICE IN MONTANA.

Billy's jaw dropped. "I knew Jed King! He was one of the finest lawmen ever to pin on a badge. He only retired about five years ago."

"I know that," Longarm said quietly.

"He must have died," Billy said. "And Chester King must have been his son."

"Or maybe a relative that he left the watch to." Longarm's eyes narrowed. "But more to the point, why was Chester murdered?"

"For his wallet, I suppose."

Longarm drummed his fingers on the top of his desk. "Didn't you work with Jed King when you started out in your federal law career?"

Billy nodded.

"And didn't he save your life in Montana during the height of that savage range war?"

"Yes," Billy said, looking out the office window, his

eyes going distant. "I was only twenty and green as the Montana grass. One of the hired gunmen tricked me into an ambush. I would have been gunned down ten miles south of town and buried, if not for Jed racing to save my hide. As it was, we still had quite a gun battle. Jed was as fine a rifle shot as I ever met. One by one, he picked off the hired killers although we were vastly outnumbered."

"Yeah," Longarm said, "I remember you telling me that story. I wish I'd have known Jed."

"He broke the mold," Billy said, shaking his head sadly. "I got a Christmas card from him the year after he retired and then . . . then nothing. I was just hoping he was a poor letter writer but was enjoying his well deserved retirement. He'd talked about moving to California. The cold Montana winters were really starting to make his bones ache."

Longarm picked up the watch and hefted it. "It's a valuable timepiece," he said. "And before I turn all this over to the authorities I thought you might like me to make a few inquiries."

"About Jed or Chester who had possession of his watch?"

"Both." Longarm's brow knitted with concentration. "Or, we can just let it go and never learn what happened to old Jed and why Chester was so brutally murdered in broad daylight. Because, frankly, it doesn't make sense that he'd be selected at random."

"Why not?"

"Chester was well dressed," Longarm replied, "but he didn't look especially prosperous. Not like some of the older gentlemen you see parading around this town with silver tipped canes and two-dollar cigars. Furthermore,

Chester was still relatively young. Perhaps in his mid-thirties so he wasn't a man that would appear to be an easy mark for muggers."

"You're reaching," Billy said.

"Am I?" Longarm smiled, but there was no warmth in it. "If you really believe this was just a random murder then I'll go over to the sheriff's office and give them these personal belongings."

"You should already have done that."

"Yeah," Longarm said, "but I wanted you to know about it first."

Almost as if he were compelled by loyalties from his past, Billy's hand reached out and closed around the gold pocket watch and chain. "I remember reading about when Jed received this watch from the Governor of Montana. On that day I'll bet that he was the proudest man on the face of the earth. The Jed King I once knew would never have surrendered this watch while he could draw a fresh breath of air."

"So don't you want to know what happened to him and who Chester was?"

Billy stared hard at the massive gold pocket watch. "I'm not sure I do, Custis. It can't help but be a tragic story."

"Since when have we shied away from bad news, boss?"

Billy managed a half smile. "Never. And . . . and I do owe it to Jed to at least make some inquiries and ensure that this watch returns to the right hands. I can't recall if Jed had a wife or not. He was quite the ladies man in his younger days. Sort of like you, Custis."

Longarm scoffed. "I just manage to get by with women. I like them and a few like me."

"Oh bosh!" Billy exploded, lightening up from his dark

thoughts. "I've never seen any man that attracted women the way you can."

Longarm shifted uncomfortably in his chair. "Let's get back to the issue of Jed and Chester King."

"All right," Billy said, placing the gold watch down on the desk. "Let's. Suppose you send a telegraph to Helena and ask their local marshal if he knows what happened to Jed and who Chester really was?"

"I've already sent the telegram," Longarm said.

"You have?"

"Yes. I'm going over to the telegraph office at noon and see if we've got a reply. Want to come along . . . for the sake of an old friend?"

"I believe I will," Billy answered. "In fact, I wouldn't miss it for the world. Jed King made a lot of enemies in the line of duty and there were plenty of men in federal prisons who had vowed to kill him when they were released. If one of them carried out that threat, it would be up to us . . . not some local lawman . . . to right the wrong."

"It would be," Longarm said in agreement.

"And, if some of Jed's most vicious enemies also had vowed to wipe the whole King family off the face of this earth, we'd have an even greater obligation to go to their aid."

"I couldn't agree more."

Billy was getting passionate now. "There's no legal authority for us to go to Montana, but there is a *moral* authority. A bond among lawmen that they should protect one another's families from harm created by their actions in honorable duty."

"There is that," Longarm said.

"Oh hell," Billy said, staring at the watch and jewelry. "Let's go down to the telegraph office right now."

15

"It's a bit soon to expect an answer," Longarm reminded his boss.

"We can wait at the telegraph office until the reply arrives from Montana."

"And what if there's no answer?"

Billy's normally congenial face hardened. "If there's no answer, then I don't think I'd be able to live with myself."

"So you'd get on the train and go all the way to Montana? Without federal authority? Without funds?"

"I would," Billy vowed. "I'd have to."

"Then you'd better count me in as well," Longarm told Billy Vail, "because it's been quite a few years since you've been out in the field and your survival instincts might be a bit rusty."

Billy paused. "If we have to go, we'd have to take an unpaid leave of absence and pay all our own travel expenses. Could you do that, Custis? I'm asking because you're always about broke."

"I could dredge up the train fare and enough extra to cover my room and meals."

"You'd do that for a man you never even knew?" Billy said.

"I knew Chester King, and he shouldn't have died like that in our town. And . . . and if there is some kind of conspiracy to murder old Jed's family . . . then you're going to need your best deputy marshal."

"Thank you," Billy said.

"You're welcome and besides, I've always liked going to Montana."

Longarm was about broke, but he knew his boss would pay the bulk of their expenses in order to solve this puzzling murder mystery.

Chapter 3

Longarm turned away from the telegraph operator and offered Billy a slight shake of his head. "I'm afraid there is still no reply from Helena."

"It's been two days!" Billy exploded. "What's the matter with the local marshal that he can't even reply with a simple telegram?"

"Maybe the marshal in Helena is just as broke as I am," Longarm answered. "Or perhaps the town doesn't even have a law officer on its payroll."

"That's impossible. Helena is one of the largest towns in Montana."

"Being the largest town in Montana isn't saying much, and the last time I was there, the cattle ranchers and sheep men were still fighting over what's left of the open grazing land. It's very possible that their law officer was either killed or else just quit. It happens all the time, Billy."

"Then let's send a telegram to the damn mayor! We need to get some answers before we go off half cocked. Has anyone claimed the body of Chester King yet?"

"No."

Billy folded his arms across his chest and asked, "Have you been able to find out what he was doing in our town?"

"Afraid not."

"Dammit, Custis, someone or something must have brought the man to Denver!"

"This is a big city," Longarm reminded his boss. "But I've finally checked with all the hotels and Mr. King wasn't registered at any of them."

"Then the man must have been staying with friends." Billy paced back and forth a moment and then said, "Let's go to the newspaper office and place an ad asking for any information on Chester King from Montana and the cause of his brutal murder. I'll add a small reward and the public can contact me right here at my office."

"That might do it. I'm sure that someone in Denver must know why he came here and why he was picked out to be assassinated in broad daylight."

"I hope so," Billy fretted.

"How long do we wait before we get on the train to Montana?" Longarm asked.

"Let's give it a week. If we've nothing by then, we'll have no choice but to go to Helena and begin our investigation."

Longarm nodded although he wouldn't have waited nearly that long before taking action. He couldn't say why, but he had a hunch that no one in this town was going to step forward with any worthwhile information on Chester King—why he'd been in town or why he'd been killed. The answers, Longarm felt sure, would only be found in Montana.

"One week, then," Billy repeated. "But I think we'll get that telegram we've been waiting for."

"I hope you're right."

"I'm optimistic," Billy said. "The mayor of Helena can't help but be familiar with someone as famous as Jed King who's a legend in that part of the West. He'll certainly be able to tell us about the famous King family. I seem to recall that Jed bought a cattle ranch . . . or was it a sheep ranch? I don't know but I remember he bought something."

"Shall I write the telegram?"

"Please do. You know how to word it properly."

"All right," Longarm said as he found a pencil and began to compose another telegram.

Their newspaper ad promising a small reward for information about Chester King appeared in Denver's leading paper the very next day. And late the following afternoon when Billy's coworkers had gone home and he was alone in his office, he received a pair of expected visitors.

"Are you Marshal Billy Vail who placed the ad in the newspaper about Chester King?" one of the large and physically imposing men asked.

Billy glanced up from the stack of government paperwork he was trying to eliminate. "I did. But how did you get into this building? It's supposed to be locked up after five o'clock."

The tallest of the pair said, "We told the security man who was just leaving for the day that you were expecting us."

"That's not true," Billy said, becoming annoyed.

"Are you the one that's offering the reward for information?"

"Sure, but . . ."

"How much?"

Billy frowned. "A hundred dollars. But the information

would have to lead to the arrest of Chester King's murderers."

"We knew Chester King . . . and his father." The taller man placed his hands on his hips and one of his fingers rested on the butt of his holstered gun. "And we know *why* Chester was here and got shot and robbed on the street."

Billy felt his heart begin to pound with excitement. "You do?"

"Yeah, but we ain't talkin' for free and we'd like to see the hundred bucks in cash before we say anything more."

Billy forgot about his stack of dull paperwork. "Gentlemen, please have a seat."

The caller said, "Who was the tall deputy that ran to Chester when he was gunned down?"

"I'll ask the questions," Billy said, trying to establish his authority. "However, if you must know, the man that tried to save Chester King is Deputy Marshal Custis Long. He works for me."

The larger of the pair drew his gun and pointed it at Billy's face. "Where can we find him *now*?"

Billy stammered, biding for time to think. "Who?"

"Deputy Custis Long!"

"Please," Billy said, raising his hands up. "Put the gun away. You're in a federal office building and I'm an officer of the law."

"An officer of the law, huh?" the shorter of the two giants asked, his voice filled with mockery. "I'd say you're nothing but a fat little pencil pusher."

Billy stared into their eyes wondering if they really would kill him at his desk. The more he looked, the more he thought they might because they had as much mercy in their eyes as a pair of rattlesnakes.

Suddenly, one of the men grabbed Billy by his shirt-front and he struggled helplessly, crying, "Let go of me!"

"Where's Chester King's wallet and other belongings," the man hissed. "He had to be carrying papers."

Billy tried to beat down his rising panic. "I'll have you arrested unless you let go of me this instant!"

The man punched Billy's face knocking him out of his chair and spilling him over backward in a quivering heap. Billy was not physically imposing and he was past his prime, but he'd once been a respected marshal and he still had a little fight left. His head felt like a melon that had been dropped from an upper story window to splatter on the pavement. Billy doubted if he'd ever been struck so hard and he knew that he was in for the worse punishment.

"Help!" he shouted as he was dragged erect and then smashed to the floor again. They started kicking him as he lay writhing in pain until somehow Billy surged to his feet and staggered for the door, but they were on him like two huge cats.

"Now," the bigger one said, his knee pressing hard against Billy's chest, "where is Chester's King's papers and personal stuff?"

"In . . . in my desk. Right upper drawer. But—"

The shorter man kicked Billy in the ribs and he felt them crack as he screamed in agony. He started to lose consciousness, but somehow fought that off long enough to hear the pair say, "The papers ain't here. Just Chester's watch and a ring."

"Then he must have left them wherever he was staying . . . or else that tall marshal named Custis Long has 'em."

• • •

Billy's ribs were broken, his lips were smashed and he was fading in and out of consciousness, but the pair hauled him erect and hustled him over to his second-story office window.

Pulling his curtains aside, one of them hissed, "Listen to me, Pencil Pusher!"

Billy tried to curse them, but choked on his own blood.

"You got one chance not to take a long dive from this window. And that's by telling us where that deputy lives."

Billy knew they would definitely ambush and kill Custis if they caught him by surprise either coming or going from his apartment. He stared down at the street below knowing his body would make a hell of a mess on the sidewalk but also knowing he couldn't live with himself if he set Custis up for an ambush. "Go to hell!"

"All right, we'll see if you can fly."

"If you do that," the other intruder argued, "he'll spatter and we'll have a hard time escaping this federal building. We got lucky gunning Chester down . . . our luck might not hold a second time."

There was a pause during which Billy stared at the sidewalk far below and knew his fate was being decided. Then one said, "He's seen our faces so we can't let him live. I'll cut his throat and be done with it."

"Good idea."

Billy struggled with all his might but he was only half conscious and no physical match for either of the two big and ruthless killers. "Please," he begged. "I *know* about the papers that Chester King had on his body when he was shot. I'm the only one that can get them for you."

"Then do it right now."

"All right," Billy muttered. "But I can't breathe.

22

Please, let me sit down and catch my breath."

They released him. Billy staggered over to his desk chair and collapsed. He bit his own smashed lip hard to sharpen his senses and then reached into his drawer for a hidden derringer. Five years before, he'd been threatened in this office by a maniac and vowed never again to be so helpless. But the derringer held only one bullet.

No matter. Billy figured he was a dead man either way so he reached into his drawer, closed his hand on the derringer and cocked it while it was still concealed. Both men were hovering over him like giant birds of prey.

"Hurry up!" one of them bellowed with impatience, starting to knock Billy's hand aside and reach into the drawer.

"Sure thing," Billy said, dragging out the little pistol, shoving it into the man's body and pulling the trigger.

The explosion was shockingly loud. The man who took the derringer's slug howled like a kicked dog as he staggered backward with shock and horror.

"Fagan, he . . . he killed me!"

Billy tried to move but was struck so hard he toppled over backward into total darkness.

Six blocks away, Longarm and a lusty young woman with long blond hair named Loretta were making passionate love. They had started their wild coupling on the bed but then had rolled onto the floor. Loretta was moaning and Longarm was pumping for all he was worth.

"Custis! Oh, Custis!" she cried. "Please stop for a moment!"

"Why?"

"Because I'm lying on your shoe and it's digging into my back!"

"Oh, hell," he panted, trying to reach under her and remove the shoe. But Loretta was a big woman and with both of their weights pressing down on the floor, he couldn't get the damn shoe free.

"Roll over," he ordered.

Loretta rolled and Longarm gasped as she bent his impaled manhood almost to the point of snapping. "Loretta, you're . . ."

But then she was on him squarely and her immense breasts were in his face effectively muffling his protest.

"Buck like a wild stallion!"

Longarm was drenched with her copious sweat, and Loretta was pounding up and down on him with such exuberance that his upstairs floorboards were protesting. He supposed that sweet old couple who lived downstairs were probably wondering if two bodies were about to crash through their ceiling.

"Buck, Custis! Buck!" she cried over and over.

Longarm grabbed Loretta by her ample buttocks and rolled her back over so that he was on top and could breathe again. He gave Loretta all he had and just when he thought that might not be enough, she began squealing like a tickled sow. It was a high, trembling squeal that carried out through Longarm's upstairs window causing pedestrians to wonder what on earth was happening in the upstairs apartment.

Longarm filled Loretta with great spurts of his seed and the woman threw her massive legs straight up in the air and then bit him on the shoulder so hard she drew blood. "Oh Custis," she moaned, wide hips still jerking with powerful contractions. "Oh my lovely big boy, what a fine coupling we had! You are the best!"

Longarm appreciated the compliment, but now that the

24

delicious deed was done, he wished Loretta would release him. He heard weak shouts from the tenants down below and called back, "It's all right, Mr. Higgins! I was . . . I was just moving furniture again!"

The weak shout became an angry oath revealing that the kindly old couple didn't believe him. Custis untangled himself from the heavily perspiring Loretta and managed to gain his footing.

"Loretta," he said, retreating from the bed. "I'm leaving for Helena."

"But not for a few days!"

He managed to reach the bed and replied, "Well, I have to leave *now*."

She launched herself at him in a rush of pure exuberance and smothered his lips with kisses. "My darling, if you have to go, I'll wait. I'll wait as long as it takes! Don't worry about me needing another man. You're the only one that can make me turn into a wanton beast!"

Longarm swallowed hard and knew that Loretta really loved him.

"That's great news," he gasped, "but I've got to start packing."

"Oh my big bucking stallion, can't it wait for just one more hour while we do a farewell dance of love?"

"Loretta," he said, trying to keep the pleading out of his voice, "I really need to go."

"Once last time, big boy. That's all I ask."

"All right," he agreed, "but I need a glass of whiskey and a few minutes to recover."

Loretta waddled over to the nightstand where he had a bottle of rye whiskey. She snatched the bottle up and took a couple of long, shuddering gulps. Then, Loretta swayed seductively over to the bed, shook her massive breasts enticingly and licked the neck of the whiskey bottle as if it were his nearly broken manhood.

Longarm managed a grin and reached for the bottle. He just wasn't a bit sure if he would survive the next hour.

Chapter 4

On his way to work, Longarm stopped by the telegraph office hoping that they might finally have some news from Helena, Montana regarding Jed King or his son Chester.

"As a matter of fact," the telegraph operator said, handing Custis a message, "this just came over the wire. I'm not sure that it's the news that you and Marshal Vail were expecting or hoping for, but here it is."

Longarm read the telegram almost in a single, hurried glance. It was from the mayor of Helena and the message was both brief, and chilling.

JED KING FATALLY AMBUSHED IN APRIL. NO
SUSPECTS. OLDEST KING SON JOHNNY DROWNED
WHILE CROSSING RIVER IN MAY. YOUNGEST SON,
CHESTER, MISSING. MIDDLE SON AND A DAUGHTER
UNDER SUSPICION BUT NOT TALKING TO ANYONE.
NEW TOWN MARSHAL JIMMY ROSCOE REFUSES TO
INVESTIGATE. WE NEED FEDERAL INVESTIGATION
AND HELP!

The telegraph operator saw Longarm's brow crease and said, "It sounds like things are in a hell of a bad state up there in Montana, huh?"

"It sure does."

The telegraph operator clucked his tongue. "You know, I haven't been able to stop thinking about that telegram since it came in and I have a theory about what is wrong up there."

Longarm was in a hurry to get the message over to Billy and wasn't interested in this man's idle speculations, but he paused out of politeness and asked, "And your theory is?"

"I think that the middle son and daughter killed the rest of the family so they could have the ranch."

"Is that right."

"Sure!"

The telegraph operator was a small, bespectacled man and now he pushed back his nightshade and steepled his fingers. "Look, Marshal, I may just be a lowly telegraph tapper, but I see a lot of people every day sending messages back and forth and most of them are pretty desperate. People come in here every day and fire off pleas for help or money or beg a loved one for forgiveness. And because I see that kind of tragedy every day, I got to be a pretty good judge of character."

"I suppose you are," Longarm said absently folding the message up and putting it into his shirt pocket. "And thanks for your theory. I'll keep it in mind."

"Do that," the little man said. "And I'll bet I'm right on the money. Usually am. Reading between the lines is my specialty and my real talent. Anyone can learn the Morse code and become halfway proficient at tapping these keys, but I've gone way beyond that in this job.

Figuring out people . . . that's what makes this job so damned interesting and keeps me from quitting because the money they pay me stinks."

"Right," Longarm said, turning for the door.

"But the only thing that has me wondering, Marshal, is how that oldest King boy, Johnny, drowned in a river. I mean, he'd have to have been pretty stupid to go into a river he couldn't cross. Doesn't make sense."

"What doesn't?"

"That a local boy wouldn't have the brains not to get himself drowned in a river he probably has swum in and crossed a hundred times."

"Rivers change in the spring floods," Longarm reasoned. "Or maybe his horse spooked and threw him and then knocked him out with a flailing hoof. Things like that happen."

"Well," the telegraph operator said looking very dubious, "I suppose that could have happened but it's just too damned convenient, if you ask me. I mean, him and this poor Chester King done in while still in the prime of their lives? And the middle son and that girl . . . you watch out for that daughter . . . she and him just refusing to talk about any of the killings. And you'll notice that nothing was said about the father . . . Jed . . . being ambushed. I am almost certain that the daughter did it."

Longarm was in a hurry, but the man's theory was plausible and even likely given the few circumstances that they had received from the mayor in Helena. However, there was another possibility that the telegraph operator was overlooking.

"Revenge," Longarm said.

"What did you say?"

"I said that Jed King was a legendary manhunter and

lawman. He killed quite a few outlaws in his day and I'll bet there are dozens of inmates who still curse his name every night before they go to sleep and vow revenge when they are finally released from a cell."

"Hmm," the telegraph operator mused. "That's probably true enough, but why would they kill Mr. King's sons?"

"I've been asking myself the same question," Longarm admitted. "The only answer I can come up with is that some men are so consumed by hatred and the need for vengeance that they'd kill not only the object of their hatred but also his family."

"You don't say."

"I do say."

The telegraph operator raised his forefinger as if a beacon of light had suddenly appeared in the midst of dense fog. "Why, Marshal!" he declared, "if that's the case in Helena, then the middle son and the daughter wouldn't be murderers, but they'd be in danger of *being murdered*."

"Exactly."

"Well," the telegraph operator said, "that does put a new light on it, but I'll still hold to my theory that the daughter and middle son are the real killers."

"Me and Billy mean to go to Montana and find that out," Longarm said as he was leaving. "Now that we have this telegram, I expect we'll leave on today's train."

"I hope you do, Marshal Long. I have to say that this is one murder mystery that I won't be able to put out of my mind until you've gone there and solved it."

"We'll do our best," Longarm promised as he headed for the office knowing that he was already late for work but that Billy Vail wouldn't be upset when he saw the telegraph and read its enigmatic message.

• • •

The minute Custis entered the federal building he knew that something was terribly amiss. A small cluster of women stood over near the stairs leaning on each other and one was crying. Other deputies stood around looking pale and somber, their expressions either worried or filled with smoldering anger.

"Custis!" a deputy named Rodney called. "Haven't you heard the terrible news?"

"No. What's wrong? Why is everyone . . . ?"

"Billy was savagely beaten last night up in his office."

"What!" Longarm started to push by the man, but Rodney stepped into his path. "Marshal Vail is still alive . . . but just barely. He's at the Denver Hospital and he's unconscious."

Longarm swallowed hard, hands knotting at his sides.

"And there's more to it," Rodney told him. "There is another man up in Billy's office shot to death."

"Who is he?"

"No one knows. It looks like Billy shot him with a derringer. And we think there was an accomplice who escaped the office because Billy's door was open and there was blood smeared on the doorknob."

Longarm didn't much care for Rodney and now he pushed the deputy marshal aside and took the stairs two steps at a time as he raced up to Billy's office. There were three other officers in the room and they were huddled together by the open window talking in low voices.

Longarm went over to the body and stared down at the dead man with his jaw clenched and his lips pressed together in a tight line.

"Custis, do you recognize that man?"

"Yes. He is one of the men that shot Chester King to death on Colfax."

The three investigators broke their huddle and rushed over to Longarm. "Are you positive?"

"I am. No question about it."

"Then the third person in this room who escaped must have been . . ."

"The partner who also shot Chester King," Longarm said, finishing the man's sentence. "Any identification on this body?"

"I'm afraid not."

Longarm bent down beside the big man and rifled his pockets. "He didn't have anything on him?"

"A gun and a knife. Some money. Fifty-six dollars, I think."

"Yeah," the other man said. "And change."

Longarm tore the dead man's coat off hoping to find a tailor's tag, but the clothes were cheap and unmarked as were the rest of the man's clothing. Longarm looked up at the trio and asked, "Where is Billy's derringer?"

"We found it under the desk. It's back in his drawer. Too bad it wasn't a double-barreled weapon. Maybe then Billy would have shot both of the men who visited him last night."

"It wasn't last night," Longarm said. "Billy never stayed at his desk past seven o'clock. Have his wife and children been notified?"

"Yeah. They're at his side right now."

Longarm studied the dead man one last time because he didn't intend to visit him at the morgue. He noted that the victim was about his own height, six-foot-four, but probably twenty pounds heavier. He also saw that the man's palms were not callused so that eliminated the idea that he was an everyday laborer. Other than that, there was nothing interesting to note.

Longarm studied the three investigators and asked, "Did anyone see this man or his accomplice enter the building after it was closed at five o'clock?"

"No."

"Or saw a man exit?"

"There are no witnesses."

Longarm moved over to the open window. He noted blood smeared on the sill and it came to him suddenly that the pair of big men must have threatened to throw Billy out the window to his death. Why? For information, of course. But *what* information?

"Custis, what are you thinking?" a man asked.

Longarm didn't answer just yet. He turned and stared down at the papers on Billy's desk and noted a bold message that read, FIND OUT IF JED KING IS ACTUALLY DEAD. HELENA, MT.

And just as important, he saw that there was a smear of blood on the note that Billy had written. It seemed plenty obvious that Billy had been beaten and almost murdered because of Jed King.

"Dammit, Custis, what!" one of the three lawmen demanded. "If you know something, tell us?"

"I don't know anything," Longarm said, not really lying to his fellow officers. "But I mean to find the answers to all of this."

"Billy might not survive the beating he took in this office. He was barely breathing when he was found early this morning. If he dies—"

"He *won't* die," Longarm snapped.

"But he might," the man insisted. "Billy isn't a kid anymore. And, if he does cash in his chips, we've got no witnesses and no answers."

33

Longarm took one last look at the dead man and turned to leave. "I'll see you later."

"You going to the hospital now?"

"That's right."

"We'll go with you."

"I'd rather go alone." Longarm softened his voice when he reached the office door. "Listen," he told them, "I know you boys feel as bad and want the answers to this crime as much as I do. But I'm taking over this case. I'll find out who that dead man is and I'll find out who was with him and escaped. And last of all, I'll learn why they came and did this to Billy."

One of the investigators said, "It wouldn't hurt if one of us helped in the investigation. In fact," he added, looking at the other two, "we're going to have to insist that we have a hand in this, Custis. You're not going to do this alone."

"Fine," Longarm told them. "Start your investigation. Right on Billy's desk is a report I wrote describing what I saw and remember regarding the shooting and murder of Chester King. Read my report and then start searching for the man whose description is included. He looks a lot like this dead man."

"That's not giving us much. What else do you know?"

For just a fraction of a second, Longarm considered giving these men the telegram that he'd just received from Helena, but then he changed his mind. The telegram had been Billy's idea and he'd share the information with Billy first. And, if Billy did die, then Longarm would go to Montana at his own expense. He'd get to the bottom of these murders and then he'd remove his badge and he'd kill every last sonofabitch that had anything even remotely to do with the death of his boss and dearest friend, United States Marshal Billy Vail.

Chapter 5

Even though he'd steeled himself for the worst, Longarm wasn't emotionally prepared for the sight of Billy lying in a hospital bed with his face beaten to a bloody pulp. He had to grab the edge of the bed and squeeze it hard with both hands to quell the sudden fury that he felt inside.

A doctor appeared and stood beside Longarm and said, "Marshal Vail's family just left for a brief spell. They were pretty upset and I thought it would be best for them to get some fresh air and calm down."

"I understand," Longarm said, never taking his eyes off his battered friend. "How is he doing?"

"As well as can be expected."

Longarm didn't like that answer. "And exactly *what* can we expect?"

The doctor was in his fifties, intelligent looking and concerned. "I am guardedly optimistic that Marshal Vail will survive. It doesn't appear that his spleen or any other vital organs were ruptured, but it's clear that he has many broken ribs. Actually, it's quite surprising that he doesn't seem to have any internal bleeding. But we can't be sure of that for a while."

"And his head?"

The doctor rubbed his own head with both hands and was slow to answer. "His face is badly swollen. Nose fractured. Cheek fractured. Jaw bruised but not fractured as far as we can tell. I suspect he has a severe concussion. There is blood in his ears and his pupils are dilated."

"Brain damage?" Longarm dared to ask.

"I can't even offer an opinion. His pulse is much stronger than when he arrived, but as you can see, his breathing remains shallow and rapid. I think that has a lot to do with the broken ribs accompanied with some obvious lung bruising. Given this man's age and general lack of fitness, he is lucky to still be alive."

"Billy doesn't look very fit or especially healthy," Longarm told the physician, "but he has a strong constitution. I'm sure you've seen the bullet wounds on his person, and he didn't survive those by being in delicate health."

The doctor nodded with understanding. "Your point is well taken and I will mark that in my medical notes. This matter of 'constitution' is vastly underrated. And it's immeasurable. No one can predict a person's will to live or innate physical strength that has nothing to do with size or musculature. Small, weak-looking men can be deceptively strong, possessing a tremendous will to live while big men like yourself who look to be in peak physical condition can sometimes just give up and die quite without medical explanation."

"Billy will live and he'll recover," Longarm promised. "But you have no idea when he might regain consciousness?"

"It could be a few hours from now . . . but it also could be weeks or even months. The body works its own miracles at its own pace. However, if I were to guess, I would say days. There is obviously brain swelling and he will have to weather that storm before he regains consciousness."

"I see." Longarm laid a big hand on the doctor's shoulder. "Just give him the best care that you can."

"I most certainly will," the man promised. "As will all the staff here at the hospital."

"Give me a minute alone with him."

"Of course."

When the doctor was gone, Longarm sat down in a chair beside Billy and took his friend's limp hand. "Billy," he pledged, "my heart wants me to stay right here by your side and watch you recover. And to be whatever comfort I can be to your wife and children. But I know that I need to catch a train for Montana and get to the bottom of this trouble. And I also know that is what you'd order me to do if you were conscious and able. So I'll be leaving you in good hands, my friend. I'll find the man that left your office and I'll find out why he did this to you and to Chester King."

Longarm stood up to go. "I'll be back as soon as I can. I am almost broke, but I'll find the train fare and enough money to do what it takes. And when I get to Montana, I'll do what's necessary and the law be damned."

So saying, Longarm left the hospital room looking neither left nor right. His mind was totally focused on finding the man that had almost killed Billy. However, before that murdering bastard died screaming, Longarm intended to get his answers . . . one way or the other.

But what he needed to do was to find some travel money.

The first place he went was to see Norman at the Blue Heron Saloon. Norman was well fixed and he'd lent Longarm money when he was in need quite a few times. Norman knew Longarm would always repay him on time with his next federal paycheck.

"How much do you need this time?" the saloon owner asked.

Longarm's mind had been too occupied by the thought of poor Billy to have given the question much consideration. "I need to go to Montana and solve a case."

"What kind of case?"

"To find out who murdered Chester King and almost beat my boss Billy Vail to death last evening."

"I hadn't heard about Marshal Vail. I'm sorry."

"Not as sorry as the man who did it is going to be," Longarm promised.

Norman frowned. "Custis, I believe you and I sympathize. But Montana is a hell of a long way off. And you'll need quite a bit of money when you arrive, right?"

"I will," Longarm agreed. "I'll probably need to buy or rent a horse, saddle and provisions. I'll be staying at hotels and eating in restaurants. I don't like to stay in bad places and eat bad food."

"And you'll want to have a few drinks and cigars."

"That's right, Norman."

"So how much money do you need?"

"At least two hundred dollars," Longarm decided. "I'll spend no more than I have to on this case, but I won't quit until it's solved and justice is done."

"You could be gone a month or more."

"True. On the other hand," Longarm said, "I might get lucky and wrap it up in a matter of days."

"I somehow doubt that," the saloon owner said. "Look. I'm a little short of cash right now but I can go you one hundred and fifty dollars."

"Thanks," Longarm said. "How much interest?"

Norman managed a smile. "You're a high-risk borrower, Custis. You seem to attract danger. For that reason alone I have to ask for fifty dollars in interest."

"You're a thief, Norman."

"I know and it pains me every day and every night."

It was Longarm's turn to smile. "What bullshit that is! All right. One fifty now and I'll repay you two hundred."

"Deal," Norman told him as he went to get the cash.

Longarm intended to go to bed early and be refreshed the next day when he boarded the northbound train, but Loretta came calling.

"Thank heavens I caught you before you left!" she exclaimed, with a big smile. "I need a little farewell loving before you go."

"And I could use some extra cash," Longarm said, keeping her from barging through his doorway.

"How much?" she asked, smile slipping.

"Fifty dollars will do."

"A loan?"

"No," Longarm said. "A gift. Loretta, I'm beat and I've got a lot on my mind. So if you . . ."

"Oh, dammit, big boy, you're worth every cent of fifty dollars. Let me in!"

Longarm sighed. He really wasn't in the mood for Loretta tonight but the extra fifty would come in handy and . . . and well, a man on the road never knew when he'd get his next tumble with an eager woman like Loretta.

She barreled through his doorway tossing her dress then underclothing in all directions. "Well," she demanded, "what are you just standing there for? Get undressed you big, handsome dog, you!"

"First the fifty dollars," he said, palm outstretched.

Loretta stomped her foot down on the floor with unconcealed exasperation. "Custis, honey, you are acting just like a big old whore!"

Longarm laughed and reached for a bottle of whiskey. Loretta might have a point here but she was the one in need while he was just tired and eager to get to Montana. That being the case, he *deserved* the fifty dollars and Longarm was sure that Loretta would get her money's worth long before morning.

Longarm was exhausted early the next morning when he left a good-bye note to the slumbering and insatiable Loretta. The note just said that he was going to the office and then directly to the train and that she needn't bother to meet him there to say good-bye. He'd miss her and return to Denver as soon as possible.

With his valise in hand and borrowed travel money in his wallet, Longarm had just locked his door and was turning around when he came face to face with a man of about his own age.

"Are you Marshal Custis Long?"

"Maybe. Who are you?" he asked, wondering if this might be someone sent to kill him.

"I'm Dr. Everett. I just left the hospital. Mr. Vail has regained consciousness and very much wants to see you."

Longarm relaxed. "Good! How's he doing?"

"Much better, but it will be months before he is fully

recovered. Mr. Vail took a savage beating. Now that we know he will live, we need to keep a close watch over his daily rate of progress . . . especially his mental activity."

"You think he might have some permanent brain damage?"

Everett was slow answering. "It is possible given the severity of his cranial injuries. But I also believe we have reason to hope that his recovery will be permanent although there might be some serious mental anguish he has to deal with."

"Billy is strong. He'll handle that part."

"We hope so. But people who have been terrorized as badly as Mr. Vail often have serious mental health problems and difficulty sleeping . . . sometimes nightmares that last for years."

"Let's go," Longarm told the doctor.

In five minutes, he was standing beside Billy and the sight wasn't very pretty. Billy's face was heavily bandaged and his eyes were purple slits. When he spoke, his swollen and discolored lips barely moved.

"Billy," Longarm whispered, laying his hand on his friend's shoulder. "Who did it?"

"Same two that you described as having murdered Chester King."

"You killed one of them and I sorta know what the other looks like," Longarm said. "Maybe I should try to find him before I go to Montana."

"No. He'll find you in Montana."

"What!"

"Custis, they demanded to know where you lived, but

I never told them. However, I . . . I gave them your name."

Longarm could see tears fed by guilt spring from the slits that were Billy's eyes. "It's all right. The killer knows what I look like and I know what he looks like. Big man, right?"

"Yeah. Looks a lot like the one that I shot up in the office."

"I'll get him," Longarm vowed. "I hope he's on the same train that I'm boarding for Cheyenne and then trans- ferring on the Union Pacific bound for Montana. I'll search every car as soon as the train pulls out of the Den- ver station."

"Try to take him alive," Billy croaked. "Custis, make every effort to find out what this is all about!"

"I will."

Billy looked up at him and his lips quivered with emo- tion. "They . . . they really worked me over, didn't they?"

"Yeah," Longarm said honestly, "but you still got the best of them."

"I did?"

"Sure. They only beat you to a pulp, but you shot one of them dead."

Billy grinned painfully. "Yeah! I hadn't thought of it that way. But you know, they almost threw me out of my window. I looked down at the sidewalk and I could just imagine my—"

"Forget about that," Longarm interrupted.

It was obvious that nearly being tossed out of the second-story window wasn't something Billy could easily forget. "I was so scared I thought I soiled my pants, Cus- tis."

"Just put it out of your mind, Billy. It will never happen again."

"I sure hope not." Billy grabbed Longarm's sleeve. "I won't rest easy until the one that got away is either dead . . . or locked up in prison."

Longarm nodded with understanding. "I prefer dead."

"So would I," Billy admitted, "but we need some answers to what happened to Chester and his family up in Montana."

"I'll get those answers," Longarm vowed, "but right now, I'd better catch the northbound train to Cheyenne."

"What about travel money?"

"I borrowed some last night."

"How much?"

"Enough."

"For you there is never enough," Billy said. "My wallet is over on the counter. Should have about seventy dollars. Take it all."

"I'm okay, Billy."

"Custis, do as I say and take the money. You always spend more than any other deputy I send out."

"That's because I get more done," Longarm reminded him.

"You're right," Billy agreed as he tried but failed to shake hands good-bye.

"So long, boss," Longarm said, "I expect you to be back at your desk and fully recovered when I return from Montana. With any luck at all, I'll return within a month."

"I'll be looking forward to it. Just watch out for that big man. He's desperate to kill you."

Longarm chuckled but it was a dry, brittle sound. "Not half as desperate as I am to kill him," he said as he left the room and headed for the train station wondering if he

43

could get all the way to Helena in less than one week.

His mind was churning as he walked the streets of Denver on his way to the railroad station. He figured he'd be two weeks coming and going to Montana and then another two weeks at least spent on the murder case. That should be enough. And during that time, he had a feeling there would be some hot lead flying and that at least one big man was going to die.

Longarm sure hoped it wasn't himself.

Chapter 6

Longarm boarded the 106-mile long Denver Pacific Railroad that would take him up to Cheyenne where he'd then buy a ticket west on the Union Pacific. As he settled into his coach seat and watched the train pull out of the Denver Station, he couldn't help but wonder if Billy Vail would make a fully recovery. Rarely had he seen a man as beat up as his poor boss.

"Morning, Marshal Long," the conductor said, punching his ticket. "Goin' out again so soon?"

"That's right, Moses. I'm headed for Cheyenne and then I'll go all the way to Helena, Montana."

Moses was a tall, somber-looking man in his sixties who always saw the dark side of things and looked as if he'd just lost his best friend or favorite dog. He was kindly and efficient, however, and had been the conductor on this train for as many years as Longarm could remember. Now, he handed Longarm back his ticket and said, "I never been to Montana. Never wanted to go there, either."

"Why not?"

"Why, Marshal Long, there are still thousands of wild Indians up there in Montana and they all hate us white men!"

"They've got good reasons not to like us much," Longarm opined. "But the Cheyenne, Crow and the Sioux are pretty much all settled on reservations and I can't imagine them going back on the warpath."

"Maybe they are peaceable today, but what about tomorrow?" Moses raised his eyebrows in question. "Marshal Long, you had better keep your scalp knotted down tight up in that wild country. All they got are cattle and Indians and a few stupid cowboys. Maybe a few buffalo hidin' out so they won't get shot. Not much else there, I hear."

"Moses," Longarm told the man, "you've got things all wrong. Montana is one of the most beautiful territories in the whole United States. It's got the finest grasslands I've ever seen and water everywhere."

But Moses wasn't buying it. "Montana is always cold. I hear that it starts snowing in September and it don't stop until the following June. That gives you just July and August to warm up before you start to freeze your butt off again. No sir. That's not for me. When I retire, I'm headed for Arizona where it's always warm and sunny. Makes an old man's bones feel good."

"Arizona is one of my favorite places except in the summer. But, Moses, I have to tell you that Yuma, from June to September is as close to hell as I ever want to get in this lifetime."

Moses started to pass on to collect tickets in the other cars when Longarm plucked his sleeve and lowered his voice. "Say, I'm looking for a big man with a black beard that could be on this train."

The conductor frowned. "Is he a friend or a foe?"

"A foe."

"A bad, bad hombre?"

"The worst kind of killer."

Moses shook his head and wrung his bony hands. "Lordy, Marshal Long, we sure don't want you killin' nobody on this train. If the bullets start to flyin', no tellin' who gets hit."

"I don't often miss with my aim," Longarm assured the man.

"But there are lots of folks on this train, and if the bullets started flyin', you never know but what somebody loses their head and jumps up in our line of fire. No sir, Marshal Long, we sure don't want no gunfight on my train."

"Moses, you have to trust me on this. All I want you to do is to check out the passengers from one end of this train to the other. If you see *anyone* that matches my description, just come back and tell me. I'll either arrest him without a fuss, or I'll shoot him dead without anyone else getting hurt."

"Don't want no dead bodies on my train. I don't like cleaning up blood. Don't like to touch the stuff. And I still say that you could miss and kill some innocent passenger. Then I would be held responsible. I might even lose my job!"

"Settle down!" Longarm told the man but to no avail.

"Then where would Old Moses be? Sitting on the sidewalk with a tin cup in his old hands beggin' for food and money! Nobody gonna hire me at my age if I let you shoot an innocent passenger . . . even if it was a mistake. And what happens if he kills you instead of you killin' him!"

Moses struck his forehead with the back of his hand. "Uh-uh, Marshal Long. I can't have none of that bloody business on my train."

Longarm had to swallow his rising impatience. "Moses," he said in a slow, deliberate voice. "I promise you I won't fire a shot. I'll just come up behind and whack the man in the back of the skull, then drag him back into the baggage train where we won't upset anyone."

Moses chewed on that for about five seconds and then asked, "But what if this man is sitting in one of the cars behind you? Now how is that gonna work? He'd see you comin' up the aisle and draw his gun and you'd have to do the same and then we'd have blood everywhere! Mess up the seats and everything!"

Longarm had to take a couple of deep breaths. He had never asked Moses for any favors and he'd never ask again. "Look," he said, "just tell me if a man matching the description I gave you is on this train. If he is, and he's sitting in a coach behind me, I'll wait until we get off at Cheyenne before I try to make my arrest. Is that fair enough?"

Moses nodded after a long, reflective pause. "You give me your word on that, Marshal Long?"

"You got my word."

"All right, then. I'll look for your man. If I see one that looks like he might be the one you want, shall I ask him for his name and where he's going?"

"Better not," Longarm said. "That could make him suspicious."

"Fine with me. I don't want no trouble on my train."

Moses left and was soon in the next coach forward. Longarm shook his head and then tipped his hat down as he settled deeper into his seat. The coach he was riding was nearly empty and that was good. Maybe he could get a little sleep before that contrary Moses returned with some news.

"Marshal Long!"

Longarm awoke with a start. "Yes, Moses?"

"There's a big, big man two coaches behind this one."

"Does he have a black beard?"

"Yes he does. There's other men on this train that have black beards, but none so big as this one or so tough looking."

"Did you speak to him?"

"I was afraid to. I just punched his ticket and he didn't say a word. But he has real mean eyes and a big scar on his cheek and I sure wouldn't want to make him mad at me."

"He might not be my man," Longarm said. "You keep an eye on him."

"I can't do that! I got a train full of passengers to take care of."

"Just keep an eye on him whenever you're passing through that coach. If he falls asleep, let me know."

Moses drew his thin shoulders back. "You promised to wait until he gets off at Cheyenne since he's in a coach behind you."

"If he's asleep, I've got to arrest him on the spot. I'll just tap him on the skull with the butt of my pistol should he become troublesome."

Moses looked very uneasy so Longarm gave him two dollars. "All right, Marshal," he finally said. "I'll keep an eye on the man. If he goes to sleep, I'll come and get you."

"Fair enough," Longarm said, managing a smile. "Is he alone?"

"Yes."

"Is his coach a lot fuller than this coach?"

"I'm afraid so."

"Well," Longarm said, "that's not good but it can't be helped. If he falls asleep, I'll take him without a shot being fired."

When the conductor disappeared again moving up the train, Longarm waited a few moments and then he eased his derringer out of his vest pocket and made sure that the weapon was ready to use. The hide-out derringer was unique and deceptive. Across his chest Longarm wore a gold chain that was connected to his Ingersol railroad watch. What was special was that instead of a fob being attached to the other end of the chain, Longarm had a solid brass, twin-barreled derringer soldered in place. He had often used the .44 caliber two-shot derringer as his "ace in the hole" to apprehend criminals who thought he was just reaching for his pocket watch but instead produced the deadly little pistol. And to make things even better, its caliber exactly matched his Colt Model T, which he wore high up on his left hip, butt forward.

"Guess I'm as ready as I can be," Longarm muttered to himself as he stood up and adjusted his coat so that it hid both weapons. The man he was after might very well be already coming up the aisle with every intention of killing Longarm.

"Always better to take the initiative," Longarm said to himself. "He who shoots first usually lives to shoot another day."

Longarm forced a smile and started down the aisle bent on taking his man alive and finding out what was behind the Montana murders.

Chapter 7

As he entered the coach where the murder suspect was sitting, Longarm drew his six-gun and slipped it under his jacket so that it would not be visible to the passengers. He paused at the head of the coach and took his time studying the people seat by seat.

There he is! About the seventh seat back on my right. His head is down on his chest and I think he is dozing.

Longarm took a deep breath and slowly started down the aisle. The closer he got to the man he was sure had helped murder Chester King and then nearly kill Billy Vail, the faster Longarm's heart pounded. Remember, you need to take him alive so that you can get some answers.

Longarm was halfway down the aisle when, suddenly, a pretty blond woman who looked vaguely familiar, glanced up and cried with delight, "Why Marshal Long! What a pleasant surprise to see you again!"

"Uh . . . yes it is," he stammered, "but could you . . ."

The woman came out of her seat to stand right before Longarm and as she did, he also saw the suspect's head snap erect.

"When we get to Cheyenne are you going east or west?" she asked.

The woman, whose name Longarm could not quite remember, was blocking his view, but he had the feeling that the murder suspect was already in motion. Afraid that the killer might actually open fire in the crowded railroad car, Longarm had no choice but to grab the young woman and try to wrestle her out of his line of fire.

"He's got a gun in his hand!" a matronly woman shrieked in terror. "He's going to shoot someone!"

Her scream created wild panic and as Longarm desperately tried to remove the young woman from between himself and the murder suspect, a single shot filled the railroad car. Longarm felt a slug sear his right shoulder. The blonde in his arms cried out and Longarm spun her aside and tried to raise his weapon but his arm wasn't responding to his command.

The big man was on his feet and in the aisle now. "Marshal, drop your gun or I'll kill you and anyone else who tries to interfere!"

The matronly woman's hysterical screams grew even louder and more shrill.

"Woman," the killer raged, "shut your yap!"

When the older woman didn't obey his command, the big man shot her in the chest. A scream died on her lips and she tumbled back into the seat, eyelids fluttering a moment before she died.

Longarm was enraged. "Dammit, you didn't need to kill her!"

"Don't move, Marshal, or your name is on my next bullet."

Longarm froze because the man was pointing his gun at his chest and ready to fire without the chance of missing. He knew this cold-blooded bastard would not only shoot him, but other passengers if things spun out of control. He didn't dare take the time to glance at his wounded shoulder, but he knew that he was bleeding heavily and that the shoulder was useless.

"All right," he said, dropping his pistol to the aisle.

The murderer cocked back the hammer of his six-gun. "I can kill you right here and right now, Marshal."

"Yes," Longarm agreed, "you could do that. But it would cause a riot and there must be some man in this coach brave enough to pull a gun and kill you before you could escape."

"Maybe. Maybe not."

"Please," the blonde who had inadvertently created this crisis said, "don't kill Custis. There's no need for anyone else on this train to die."

"She's right," Longarm said, raising his voice. "Everyone keep quiet and don't move. I'm a United States Marshal and I don't want to see anyone else die on this train."

"Good advice, Marshal Custis Long," the man with the gun said, offering a twisted smile that did nothing to warm the heart. His upper front teeth were missing and now that Longarm had time to study the killer for more than a split second, he could see that he also had a long, puckered and jagged scar on his left cheek. The scar ran from his ear into his beard and down to the corner of his mouth. Longarm guessed it had been caused by a bowie knife.

"So what happens now?" Longarm asked feeling a trickle of warm blood seeping down his sleeve to drip from his fingers.

"Marshal, I think we need to take a little walk."

"Where to?"

"Someplace that we can have a *private* conversation. Let's go back to the caboose."

Longarm knew it was a command and not a request. "Sure thing," he said, "lead the way."

"Ha! Very funny, Marshal. Now move."

"Please!" the blonde said, maybe realizing for the first time that she had been the one that had placed Longarm in this terrible predicament. "Can't you just leave Custis be?"

"What?"

"I . . . I mean you don't have to kill Custis or anyone else."

"Miss, you must be an idiot. I just killed that woman because she wouldn't shut her big yap. Do you want the same?"

The blonde paled. "No."

"Then shut up and don't you or anyone say another word or I'll turn this coach into a slaughterhouse."

Longarm had seen a lot of deadly and desperate men in his time but none more so than this one. Trying hard to keep his voice from carrying the fear that he was trying to override, Longarm said, "No one else needs to move or say a word. We're leaving this coach and I don't want anyone following. Just stay in your seats. Someone attend to that woman."

"She's dead," a young man with a handlebar mustache seated next to her whispered. "He shot her down as if she were a rabid dog. I . . . I swear that you will burn in hell, mister!"

The big man turned his gun and smiled. "Two loud-mouths sitting side by side as corpses. That would be something to see. Do you want to die, bub?"

"Of course not."

"Then shut up or I'll shut you up permanent like I did that old parrot slumped next to you!"

Longarm glared at the brave but foolish young man. "Do as he says and don't say another word."

"Yes, sir," the young man said, his jaw knotted and his eyes burning with hatred toward the shooter.

"All right, Marshal, put your hands over your head and move past me real slow. Don't stop until you reach the back door of this coach."

Longarm glanced aside and his eyes locked with the blonde. He still couldn't remember her name but her face was familiar, even though it was filled with regret for the mess she had caused.

"This has nothing to do with you," he told her a moment before he stepped down the aisle. "Everything will turn out all right."

"Like it did for that poor dead woman?"

Longarm didn't have an answer so he tried to raise his hands overhead, but his right one wouldn't go above his wounded shoulder.

"Higher!" the man with the gun ordered.

Longarm touched the ceiling of the coach with his left hand, but try as he might, he could not get his right one up even another inch.

"Move!" the killer ordered.

Longarm eased past the gunman and walked to the end of the coach.

"Open it, Marshal."

"I have no feeling in my right hand." He turned slightly and showed the gunman his bloody hand adding, "I think your bullet shattered my right shoulder."

"Hurt?"

Longarm saw no point in denying the fact. "Like hell."

55

The killer laughed. "All right," he said after a moment, "lower your left hand and open the door. We got one more passenger coach before we reach the caboose. If you try to escape or get help, I'll put a hole in your back big enough for a damned crow to fly through. Understand?"

"Yeah," Longarm grated.

"Good. Then let's get this over with."

Longarm didn't like the way that sounded, but he had no choice but to do as the gunman said so he opened the door, crossed between the two cars and risked a moment to glance out at the landscape that was flying by. They were nearing a little whistle-stop called Platteville where the train would often stop to take on a few passengers and sometimes water.

Would the train stop at Platteville today? Longarm didn't know but he was hoping it would. Maybe then he could leap from the caboose and somehow manage to escape.

"Keep moving!" the man with the gun growled as he shoved the barrel hard into Longarm's spine.

They went through the last passenger coach in a hurry, the gun pressed to Longarm's back every step of the way. He was relieved when they exited that passenger coach and reached the caboose.

"Open it up and don't say a word if anyone is inside."

"What do you intend to do with me?"

"Depends what you have to say, Marshal. Now, move!"

Longarm opened the door and was dismayed to see two railroad men sitting around a table playing penny ante poker.

"You men sit still and don't move!" Longarm warned.

"Say, Marshal, what's going on? Who is . . ."

The railroad man's words died on his lips when he saw that Longarm's shoulder was bloody. He started to come to his feet and then wisely changed his mind when he saw the gun come up to aim at his heart. Turning pale, he sat down again.

"You don't have to gun down these railroad men," Longarm said over his wounded shoulder. "Everyone on this train is a witness and can identify you so it doesn't matter about this pair."

"You're right," the big man agreed. "But there are just some days when I feel like killin' folks."

"These are both good family men."

"You're breaking my heart."

"At least let them jump," Longarm argued. "They can at least do that."

There was a long, heart-stopping pause and then the killer said, "You boys got two choices. Jump off the back of this train or get shot."

"But it's still rolling too fast to jump," one of the men protested.

"Do it!" Longarm shouted. "Or he'll kill you!"

The pair sprang up from the table and it was plain to see that they were scared witless. They practically ran each other down trying to get out the back door and Longarm saw them dive off the rear platform of the train.

At least they were going to live. They might break a few bones and get bruised up real bad, but they'd live, if they didn't break their necks.

"All right," the man with the gun said. "Sit down, Marshal, and let's have a little talk."

"What about?"

"Why the King family! What else?"

Longarm nodded. Talk was good. Talk would give him a little extra time to figure out how he was going to survive.

Chapter 8

Longarm rested his right hand on the table and flexed his fingers. They tingled and when he rubbed his forefinger and thumb together, he thought he felt a slight degree of numbness. In his vest pocket lay the hidden derringer, attached to his watch chain. But what were his chances of being able to snatch the little firearm up and then shoot it accurately given that his right hand was slick with fresh blood?

I might be able to do it with my good left hand, he thought, if I can get this killer to relax and lower his guard.

"So what do you want from me?" Longarm asked. "I didn't know Chester King."

"I'm sure that's true," the big man said, leaning back against the door with his gun loosely held in his fist. "But when you interfered on Colfax Street, I looked back and saw you talking to the man. I think he told you something we want to know."

"He didn't tell me anything."

The man tightened his grip on the gun. "Of course he

did. He told you where his father hid all the money."

Longarm frowned. "Jed King had money?"

"Of course he did! You don't think that he gave back all the money he retrieved from the holdups, do you?"

"I believe Jed was an honest and brave man," Longarm answered, shocked to hear that Jed might have been taking some illegal money for himself.

"Brave? Sure. That man wasn't afraid of anything that crawled or walked, but he wasn't honest. In fact, he had the habit of taking about twenty percent of every dollar he retrieved from a train, bank or stagecoach holdup."

"That's not true."

"Isn't it?" The big man sneered. "Your biggest problem is that you think every lawman is honest . . . but they sure ain't. I know for sure that, after Marshal King retired, he was secretly one of the wealthiest men in Helena, Montana. Of course, no one knew that because he didn't spend his money when he was in town. Oh no! Everyone in Helena thought Jed King was as honest as the day is long and he sure didn't want to spoil that reputation. But now and then, old hero Jed would go off to San Francisco or St. Louis and spend money like a drunken sailor."

"I don't believe a word you're saying," Longarm told the man. "And, even if it were true, I don't know anything about that money. I never once met Jed King."

"Your boss did. He knew about King but not the fact that he never turned in all the holdup money."

Longarm slipped his left hand a little closer to his vest pocket. "Is that why you beat Billy Vail half to death?"

"We thought he might know something useful."

Longarm shook his head. "Like I said before, I don't know a thing. Not about his children or about King himself."

"Too bad," the man with the gun said. "We figure that poor Chester would have confessed with his dying breath how his father managed to steal over seventy thousand dollars."

"He didn't. By the time I reached his side, he was too far gone."

The man cocked his gun and pointed it at Longarm. "I don't believe you, Marshal. I think you're lying and that's going to earn you an early grave."

Longarm could feel that his time was about to run out. "All right!" he blurted, not sure what he was going to say next but knowing the only thing that could save him were words. "Chester King did tell me some things before he died. Maybe—"

"Maybe what?"

Longarm feigned confusion. "At the time, I didn't think they meant anything. But now that you've told me about Jed King, perhaps his last words *were* important."

"What did he say?"

Longarm's brow furrowed and he gazed up at the ceiling of the caboose as if he were concentrating with all of his might. But what he was really doing was trying to keep this man's attention focused on anything but his left hand as it slipped across his belly toward the vest pocket where his derringer lay hidden.

"Young Chester King said that there was a place on the ranch that I needed to tell his brother about."

"*Which* brother?"

Longarm swallowed hard, pretending confusion. "He didn't say."

The big man swore. "He must have meant Dave. We drowned Johnny in the river because he didn't know where his pa hid his stolen money."

"Or maybe," Longarm said, "he knew you would drown him whether he told you or not where Jed's stash was hidden."

"*Where* on the ranch did Chester talk about?"

Longarm had no idea what he should say so he changed the subject. "Your name is Fagan, right?"

"How'd you know that?"

"Billy Vail heard your late friend call you Fagan while you were working him over in his office."

"It don't matter what my name is, Marshal. You either tell me where that money is hidden or you're a dead man."

"Behind the barn," Longarm blurted even as his own fingers closed on the derringer. "It's buried behind the barn."

"The hay barn or the horse barn?"

Longarm wasn't ambidextrous, but there was no choice except to yank the derringer out of his vest pocket with his left hand and fumble to pull the trigger before Fagan shot him to death.

Fagan was quicker than he appeared. For an instant, he was distracted by Longarm's talk, but then he saw the derringer start to appear and he reacted swiftly. Longarm used his useless right hand to slap Fagan's gun barrel sideways and then he fired into the big man's body. Fagan grunted and knocked Longarm aside, then charged through the door.

Longarm fired his second barrel, but the derringer was notoriously inaccurate and his second bullet bit into the door frame an instant before the killer jumped from the train. By the time that Longarm got to the rear platform, Fagan was coming to his feet and running toward a farmhouse near the tracks.

"I've got to stop him!" Longarm hissed, furious at himself for letting the killer escape. But as he stood on the platform looking for a place to leap, the train crossed a deep riverbed. There was simply no way that Longarm could jump while the train was on the bridge.

By the time that they were across the riverbed, Fagan was gone and Longarm was so weak from the loss of blood he knew he would never catch the man.

Was Fagan wounded as badly as himself? Longarm doubted it. The big man with the black beard and soulless eyes had been hit by Longarm's first bullet, but it must not have done much damage. Either that, or Fagan was inhumanly strong and too tough to kill.

Longarm staggered back into the caboose and collapsed at the table where the railroad men had been playing cards. On one of the empty seat cushions, he saw a pint bottle of whiskey they'd probably been hiding from the conductor.

Just what I need, Longarm thought as his head began to spin. He managed to grab the bottle and take a long pull. The liquor burned down his throat and it felt good but that's the last thing he remembered before he passed out from the loss of blood.

Chapter 9

Longarm woke up with a jolt while lying on a doctor's examining table with the smell of medicine on his tongue and a dull pain in his right shoulder.

"How are you feeling?" the doctor asked, as he finished bandaging Longarm's wound and then stepping back to admire his work.

"Where am I?"

"You are at the Sisters of Charity Hospital in Cheyenne, Wyoming."

Longarm swallowed and studied the doctor who was fresh-faced and smiling. He was slender with a sparse little red goatee and mustache that looked ridiculous on one so young. Longarm turned his attention to his bandaged shoulder. He wriggled his fingers to make sure that he hadn't suffered severe nerve damage.

The doctor rested his pointed chin on his right hand and said, "Any numbness when you wiggle your fingers?"

"Not anymore. There was on the train." Longarm tried to sit up but was struck by a severe attack of dizziness.

"Wow," he groaned. "The world wants to go spinning around again."

"You've lost a great deal of blood. My name is Dr. Lane. When they brought you into this hospital, you were as pale as a pond lily and your pulse was extremely weak. If it hadn't been for that young and highly skilled nurse, Miss Allison Danner, you would have hemorrhaged to death long before the train could get you to this hospital."

Longarm was covered with a sheet, and when he raised it and peeked downward, he saw that he had been undressed and was naked. "What happened to my clothes?"

"Marshal Long, I assure you that you wouldn't want them back," Dr. Lane said. "They were torn and even your pants were soaked with blood. We have your badge, papers, weapons, boots and personal belongings in a safe."

"I'd like to see them, Doctor. I had quite a bit of cash and—"

"It's all in your wallet, which is in the hospital lock up." Lane smiled boyishly. "This hospital relies heavily on charity and God knows we need more money for operating expenses, but we haven't yet been forced to resort to stealing our patient's hard-earned money while they are unconscious."

"I'm sure you haven't," Longarm replied, feeling a bit ashamed for thinking that these people would rob one of their own patients. "Say, Doc, how soon can I leave this place?"

"I want you to stay tonight, and, if you are feeling stronger and your color is improving, you can leave in the morning. However, you must confine yourself to bed rest for at least a week."

"I just can't do that," Longarm said.

For the first time, the doctor grew stern. "Marshal, I

personally removed the bullet that was lodged in your shoulder. I also picked out fragments of bone. I can assure you that, if you do not follow my recommendations, your shoulder will heal improperly and you may lose the use of it . . . permanently."

"Why?"

"Because the bones, muscles and tendons need time to heal properly. Do you want everything to work against itself? Bone grating bone?"

"Of course not."

"Then you must keep your right arm immobilized in a sling for no less than three months. After that—"

"Three months!" Longarm wailed. "That's ridiculous! Dr. Lane, I'm hot on the trail of a man who murdered an innocent pedestrian in Denver, then nearly killed my boss, then shot a train passenger for doing nothing more than making too much noise, then tried to kill me."

"He escaped," Lane said. "There's nothing you can do about that now. I'm telling you the truth, Marshal, if you don't follow my instructions, you will never regain the full use of your right arm. Is that clear?"

Longarm could see that argument would get him nowhere with this young doctor. And, while he wished he could take a month or two off to slowly recover, that was just out of the question. Fagan was on the loose and he might even try to track Longarm down and finish what he started right here in Cheyenne. At the very least, Fagan and whoever else was in with him on this murderous quest to find hidden money would return to Helena intent on digging up money behind some barn just because Longarm had lied. Failing to find that money, they'd become enraged and most likely kill off the rest of Jed King's offspring.

Longarm slid his feet off the examining table and brushed the earnest doctor aside as he attempted to stand. No one was more surprised than himself when he had to grab the table with his left hand in order to keep from falling.

"Are you finally satisfied?" Dr. Lane challenged. "Or do you want to try to reach that door but instead fall flat on your face?"

The sheet had slipped to the floor and Longarm was standing buck naked and very shaky beside the examining table. His head had begun to spin again and his legs shook with the effort to stay erect.

"All right," he whispered. "I'll rest awhile."

"More than 'a while,' Marshal. You'll rest for as long as it takes to rebuild your blood volume and strength."

"Help me lie back down," Longarm said weakly.

Lane helped Longarm back on the table and said, "We'll be moving you to a room in a few minutes. Miss Danner is there waiting."

"Is she the blond woman that blew my cover just before I confronted the killer?"

"I don't know about that. But she was on the train and did manage to staunch your bleeding until you could be brought here to surgery."

"I don't remember anything after Fagan jumped and I sat down to have a sip of bad whiskey."

"You were foolish to have that drink of liquor. It stimulated your heart and made it beat faster causing you to lose blood faster. Being a federal officer of the law and having as many old scars as you do, I'd have thought you'd have known better, Marshal Long."

Longarm was becoming annoyed with Dr. Lane and decided not to say anything more. He lay down and was just starting to relax when two white-frocked nurses and a burly orderly arrived to transfer him from the examining table to a cart with wheels. He was moved down cold and sterile-looking hospital corridors until he arrived at his room which was spartan and would have depressed him if it were not for the presence of the lovely blond woman he'd so briefly and unfortunately encountered on the northbound train from Denver.

"Custis!" she said, rushing to his side. "I'm so glad that you pulled through."

"Me too. But I'm afraid that I don't remember you."

"There's no reason that you would. But I remember you because you saved my brother's life three years ago during a bank robbery in Reno. You just happened to be there when three men came in the door and demanded money. One of them put the barrel of his pistol to my brother's temple."

"Oh yeah. I thought he was going to pull the trigger."

"He probably would have if you hadn't distracted the man and then shot him between the eyes. Not only that, but you killed both of his accomplices. The whole town was at your feet for a few days. You could have been elected mayor of the city if there had been an election. I remember that I rushed up to you and gave you a kiss on the cheek for saving Floyd."

If Longarm hadn't been short of blood, he might have blushed. "I'm glad I was there and got lucky."

"Luck had nothing to do with it," Allison Danner countered. "I wasn't in the bank, but my brother said you were the coolest, bravest man he'd ever seen . . . not to mention being the best marksman."

"Well, I'm glad it turned out as well as it did. That's not always the case, you know. Sometimes I've been in

69

fixes where innocent people lose their lives and I'm powerless to save them."

Allison smiled and touched Longarm's cheek. "You were Reno's hero three years ago and you're still my brother's hero as well as my own."

"Aw, well, aw, heck."

While Longarm fumbled for words, he was onto his bed but was embarrassed when the sheet covering him again slipped to the floor revealing him in his natural entirety.

"My," one of the nuns who was helping exclaimed. "You are covered with scars. You'd better find a safer occupation, Marshal, or the Lord will be calling you soon."

"Sister, I'll give it some serious thought," Longarm said, noticing that Miss Allison Danner was staring at something that sure had nothing to do with his scars.

When everyone but Miss Danner left the room, Longarm pulled the sheet up under his chin and tried to act as if he hadn't been exposed. "Well, Miss Danner," he struggled, "Dr. Lane says that I owe you my life for stopping the bleeding."

"It wasn't that difficult. Just good old pressure bandaging. Dr. Lane reminds me of a schoolboy, but he's an excellent surgeon. He had that bullet out of your shoulder in just a few minutes and he did a fine job of suturing."

"I'd guess him at being about fifteen years old."

"He's ten years older," Allison said. "Same age as I am. He's asked me to marry him, but I couldn't do that."

"Why?"

"Because he looks and acts like a little boy when he's not practicing medicine."

Longarm didn't know what to say about that so he kept

quiet. He was thinking about the doctor's orders that he keep his arm immobilized for three months. That, of course, was out of the question. He might make it three days but that would be all.

"Miss Danner?"

"Call me Allie. I called you Custis on the train. Remember?"

"Yes. Well, Allie, I take it that you work here?"

"That's right. I don't get paid much, but the sisters are so nice and they're shorthanded. Money really isn't all that important to me."

"Nice to hear."

"My father was Senator George Danner. I'm sure you've heard of him."

"I have," Longarm said. "I believe he passed away a few years ago."

"That's right. He was a dear man and very lonely after my mother died. He left me and my brother a ranch and quite a few head of cattle. But I had no interest in cattle ranching nor did Floyd so we sold everything and invested it elsewhere. We've been fortunate and done very well."

"So that's why you don't need a wage here at this hospital."

"Yes," she told him. "But one needs something important to do with one's life so I learned nursing and do what I can around here. I had been visiting friends in Denver and was returning to Cheyenne when the trouble on the train started. I'm sorry that I exposed your identity and got you wounded."

"That's all right."

"I overheard Dr. Lane saying that you might be able to leave the hospital tomorrow. Where will you go?"

"I've stayed at the Buffalo Hotel many times. I can stay there again."

"Oh, that's out of the question!"

Longarm frowned. "Why?"

"Because their food is awful, their sanitation leaves everything to be desired and you need constant care . . . at least for the next week or two."

"Miss Danner, I—"

"Allie," she interrupted. "And I want you to stay with me and Mrs. Grimshaw."

"Who is Mrs. Grimshaw?"

"She's a nice old lady that lost her home and fell on hard times. She is my friend and housekeeper. She is also fun to be around and a wonderful cook."

Longarm nodded. In truth, the Buffalo Hotel had become rather seedy and the food there was nothing to brag about. The hotel itself had become the last address for old buffalo hunters and bone pickers whose personal habits of spitting on the floor without bothering to go to a spittoon was a bit disgusting.

"Now don't argue with me, Custis. Mrs. Grimshaw and I will take wonderful care of you and even fatten you up a bit."

"I'm not too thin."

Allie shook her head and clucked her tongue like a spring chicken. "I don't want to embarrass you, Custis, and you must remember that I am a trained nurse so the human body is nothing new to my eyes."

"Allie, I—"

"But I *saw* you, Custis, and you are very much underweight. Don't they feed you well in Denver?"

"I feed myself and go out to dinner quite often," he said. "I eat good steaks and like potatoes and beans."

"You are still badly underweight and we'll work on that as well as building up your blood volume."

"Allie, I have to leave for Helena, Montana as soon as possible," Longarm said. "The man that shot me in the shoulder is convinced that he is on to a fortune in buried holdup money. He'll stop at nothing to get what he wants and I believe he is not acting alone. Have you heard of Jed King?"

"No."

"He was a United States Marshal and one of the best. Sorry to say, the man who had become a legend among lawmen died in Helena a few years ago. I'm afraid that his adult children are being murdered one by one. Two sons have already been murdered and there is only one son and a daughter left. I have to see and warn them and then try to stop the killing before every last member of the family is dead."

Allie's blue eyes widened. "Good grief! That's an amazing story. How sad."

"You could call it that," Longarm told her. "But what I'm trying to make you understand is that lives are on the line, and I'm probably the only one who can save two innocent people living up in Helena."

"Is that what you're doing . . . going through life saving other people's lives?"

"And my own." Longarm expelled a deep breath. "Allie, there's something else you should know and consider before you ask me to move into your house."

"Let me guess," she said, tapping her front teeth with a fingernail. "You're not at all the gentleman that you appear to be and you have no honor when it comes to the seduction of weak and kindhearted women."

Despite feeling bad, Longarm had to laugh. "You

guessed it. But I'm afraid there's more and this is serious."

"Seduction isn't serious?"

Longarm knew that she was pulling his leg, trying to get him to lighten up and he appreciated that. But he needed her to take what he had to say next seriously.

"What I'm talking about is the possibility that the man on the train will come to Cheyenne and try to finish the job on me. And, if he does, that would put you and poor Mrs. Gimshaw in grave danger."

Allie's teasing smile faded. "Do you really think that's possible?"

"Of course it is! He was on that train because I was on it and I've no doubt that he would have come looking for me if I hadn't gone looking for him first."

"I see."

"So, given that possibility, perhaps you'd like to take back your offer of hospitality."

"No," Allie said, "I wouldn't. I'm a good shot and I always have a gun by my bed at night. Mrs. Grimshaw is so imposing that she'd probably beat any attacker to death with her broom. And I assume you will keep a gun handy?"

"I will," Longarm promised. "And the other thing is, I wounded Fagan. I don't know how badly but there is a chance his wound was fatal. I won't know until I return to the place where he leapt from the train and start asking everyone in area if they saw Fagan. Or buried him."

"I hope he died and they left him to rot beside the tracks," Allie said, all of her teasing now replaced by cold anger. "What kind of a monster would gun down a woman just because she was hysterical and wouldn't stop screaming?"

"The worst kind," Longarm assured her. "The very worst."

Allie got up to leave. "I've got other patients to look after, but I'll be popping into this room every half hour or so until evening when I leave the hospital."

"Thanks."

"You're welcome," Allie said as she mustered a smile and left the room.

"Oh, Allie?"

She stopped. "Yes?"

"I want my derringer and six-gun right now."

Her eyes widened with concern. "But you're safe here."

"I'm sure you're right," Longarm said. "But I never want to be caught empty-handed and by surprise. I'll rest better if I'm armed."

"I understand," she said. "I'll talk to the head nurse and doctor."

"Don't do that," Longarm cautioned. "Just bring my pocket watch that is attached by the watch chain to my derringer. And also bring my Colt revolver. And make sure that both are loaded."

"Anything else, Marshal Long?" she asked with eyebrows upraised.

"Not that I can think of."

"What a shame!" Allie winked at him. "You need to exercise your imagination," she said, vanishing around the corner leaving Longarm to wonder what in the hell that was all about.

Chapter 10

Dr. Lane was skeptical about allowing Longarm to leave the hospital the next morning and he was downright upset when he learned that his patient was going to be recovering at Allison's house.

"That's not proper!" he protested loudly. "The whole town will be talking about this!"

"Mrs. Grimshaw is living with me so it is proper. It's no different than if I was running a boardinghouse."

"Or course it's different!"

"What are you thinking, Dr. Lane?" Allison asked. "Surely you are not . . . oh my heavens, you dirty-minded thing!"

"I'm *not* dirty minded."

"Then what is your problem? You said that Marshal Long needs a great deal of care. Mrs. Grimshaw will be with him all day and I will be with him . . . in the day when I'm not here working."

Lane's face was almost as red with anger as his scraggly mustache and goatee. "And what if he needs assistance *at night*?"

"I'm a nurse so I guess I'll just have to give him whatever aid and comfort he requires."

"Allison!"

"Herbert," she retorted. "What is the matter with you?"

"*You* are the matter with me," he said. "If you insist on doing this, your reputation as a lady of high standards and morals will be ruined in Cheyenne. And I will never condescend to take such a person as my lawfully wedded wife."

"Good," Allison said smartly. "Then I'll take that to mean that you'll stop pestering and ogling me all the time."

The doctor blanched, turned on his heels, and marched away.

"Allison," one of the nuns said in a reproving tone of voice, "you really shouldn't take that young lawman into your home. Temptation works through the Devil, you know."

"Sister Carrie, that lawman saved my brother's life and the reason he was shot is because I exposed his cover. The truth is that I owe Marshal Custis Long more than I can ever repay."

"Oh?"

"I do!"

"And do you owe him your eternal soul if you fall to temptation and fornication?"

"Sister Carrie!"

She clucked her tongue three times in sharp disapproval then turned on her heel just like Dr. Lane and marched away.

"Well," Allison muttered, "it appears that no one has given me any regard whatsoever for my strong will to fight temptation. And for that, I shall prove them wrong."

· · ·

When Longarm was brought to Miss Allison Danner's home, every neighbor on the city block was either out on the street witnessing the event as if it were a high crime, or else peeping through their windows and thinking that Miss Danner was not the proper young lady that she had always seemed to be.

Longarm was still in considerable pain and completely unaware of the stir he was causing. Grateful to be out of the hospital, he shut his eyes and allowed the strong hospital orderlies to transfer him from an ambulance wagon onto a litter. With Mrs. Grimshaw and Miss Danner at his side, he was carried into an extra bedroom and eased onto a bed with silk sheets.

"Nice knowin' you, Marshal," one of the orderlies called.

"Have fun!" the other chortled.

"I swear," Mrs. Grimshaw snapped. "I don't know what has gotten into this neighborhood! People all standing around gossiping. There must be something going on, but for the world I can't imagine what."

"Ignore them," Allison advised. Then, tucking the sheets up around Longarm's neck and puffing up his feather pillow, she introduced the old woman to Longarm and the pair studied each other closely.

Longarm considered himself an excellent judge of women all ages, sizes, dispositions and descriptions. And although Allison had already informed him that Mrs. Grimshaw had fallen on hard times and was now her housekeeper, he saw a woman with a lot of pluck and spirit. Face ravaged by worry and time, she nonetheless stood ramrod straight and her reddish nose had the aggressive shape of an eagle's beak. She was a large woman

79

but not fat and soft as most of her vintage. Rather, she walked with the rolling gait of a saloon bouncer or perhaps a tough sailor. Her hands were arthritic, knuckles large and probably stiff, but they were competent hands and powerful. She had the look of a person who had endured hard times all her life, but rather than be defeated by them, she had simply clenched her teeth and endured.

The old gal might be impoverished, Longarm thought, but life sure hasn't cowed her spirit.

"Welcome to the Danner house, Marshal Long," the housekeeper intoned, her keen eyes boring into him with neither admiration nor dislike. "I understand that you will be staying with us for a while."

"Not long."

"Well, we shall see about that. Dr. Lane said one week of complete bed rest and that's what you should do."

"Nice room," Longarm said, changing the subject as he gazed around at the yellow lace curtains, the nice pictures on the walls and the well crafted mahogany furniture and bedposts. "Very nice. I'm not accustomed to staying at such a homey and pleasant place."

"Where *have* you been staying?" Mrs. Grimshaw asked, the first hint of suspicion in her hard, probing eyes. "Not at whorehouses, I hope."

"Mabel!" Allison protested. "What a thing to say to our brave guest."

"I'm sorry, miss, but if our guest has been staying in low places, I should carefully examine his body to make sure that there are no lesions or lice. Such things can spread and be contagious."

"Mabel, good heavens!"

"Only protecting our house and home, Miss Allison."

80

"Well, please do not bring that sort of thing up again. Marshal Long—"

"Custis," he told them.

"Mabel, our guest normally stays at the Buffalo Hotel."

"Oh," Mrs. Grimshaw said, wagging her chins, "now that's a low, low place to rest one's head. And there's whores that come and go there day and night for that hotel's degenerate and drunken boarders. Is that why you stayed there, Marshal Long? For the scabby, lice and disease-infested whores?"

"Mrs. Grimshaw!" Allison protested with real outrage. "There will be no more mention of those unsavory things. Is that understood?"

"Yes, Miss Danner."

Longarm saw the hard smile on the old gal's face and knew that wasn't anything near the end to questions about "unsavory things." He also knew that he was going to have to keep his guard up around Allison's tough and suspicious housekeeper. One good thought, however, was that Allison had been correct when she'd said that Mrs. Mabel Grimshaw could probably beat Fagan to death with her broom.

At that same time, sixty-five miles south of Cheyenne near the whistle-stop at Platteville, Fagan was sitting at the table of the Knott homestead. He was in considerable pain but that was easing because homesteader Everett Knott liked his whiskey and was plenty glad to share it with a man who was paying him and his wife a dollar for the privilege of sitting at his poor supper table.

"And so," the half-inebriated Knott was saying, "our children are gone and me and the missus got to do all the work on this homestead. We work from sunup to sundown every day including Sundays. Right, Ginny Girl?"

"If you say so, Everett."

"But it ain't right, us working so hard." Knott grinned loosely at his young wife. "Of course, in the winter when it's freezin' and snow is deep on the farm, we spend a lot of our time in bed, huh, Ginny Girl?"

Knott cackled lewdly but his wife was stone-faced.

Watching them, Fagan couldn't help but wonder how this ruined sot had managed to attract and marry a wife so much younger and attractive than himself. "What happened to your children?"

"All quit the homestead and drifted away. They weren't Ginny's children. They were mine from a former marriage. My first wife died of the cholera. I'd seen it comin' for years 'cause she was always skinny and weak. Had a bad stomach and a terrible disposition. Farted day and night and they was smelly ones."

"That's hard," Fagan said.

"But she's gone and forgotten," Knot said. "And I took a new wife right away. Little Ginny Girl ain't much older than my boy, are you, gal?"

"No," the subdued woman said. "Your kids are all gone and I wish we were gone too."

Everett Knott acted as if he were hurt by this sour observation. "Now, Ginny Girl! You shouldn't be sayin' that! Our guest, Mr. . . . what did you say your name was, mister?"

"Smith. Joe Smith," Fagan lied.

"Yes, now Mr. Smith might get the wrong idea about Colorado homesteading. It ain't so bad. We don't make much money, but we got two sound horses, three pigs and a good milk cow. Not bad for only five years on this homestead. And we'll keep doin' better, won't we!"

Ginny didn't say a word except to ask Fagan how his ribs were feeling.

"They're feelin' much better." Fagan forked some more chicken into his maw and then added mashed potatoes. He couldn't believe how lucky he'd been to have the federal marshal's bullet stopped by a silver dollar resting in his vest pocket while they struggled in the train's caboose. If it hadn't been for the silver dollar, he'd be a dead man.

"Quite a bruise you had there," Knott said wiping his lips and taking another drink. "And how'd you say you got stuck way out here without a horse or nothin'?"

"I didn't say, but the horse pitched me and ran off."

Everett Knott thought that hilarious. He threw back his head and guffawed, spewing food and spittle all over his wife and guest. Then, he drank more whiskey.

"So," Fagan said, "you think my getting tossed by a horse is real, real funny, huh?"

"I sure as hell do!" Knott cried, pounding the table. "Why, I'd sell you a good horse, but we need him to pull the plow."

"What if I just decided to take the horse for free?" Fagan asked, his voice going soft and deadly.

Knott didn't get it. He stared at Fagan and shrugged. He looked at his young and comely wife as if to ask her what their guest meant. Ginny Girl was already beginning to understand. She was not bright, but she was far brighter than her drunken, homesteading husband.

She swallowed hard and plucked at her faded cotton dress. "Would you like some more chicken, Mr. Smith?"

"No," he said. "But take that jug from your drunken husband and pour me another glass."

"Yes sir, Mr. Smith."

Ginny poured and her nerves betrayed her as the jug jiggled against the rim of her guest's glass. She even spilled some of the liquor, which upset her husband, and he nearly backhanded her for being so clumsy.

In fact, he would have backhanded his Ginny Girl except for suddenly noticing a gun that had suddenly appeared in his guest's first. A gun that was pointed across the small, ugly kitchen table at his face.

"Ha! Ha!" he laughed raggedly. "You gonna shoot my wife for spillin' our whiskey?"

"No," Fagan said, "I'm going to shoot *you*."

"Ha! Ha! Ha!" Everett Knott laughed but his laugh was now shrill and hollow.

Ginny raised her hand as if trying to push Fagan's aim aside, but then she lowered it and turned to face her husband. "Bye, bye, Mr. Knott," she said without a trace of regret or emotion.

Fagan's bullet struck Everett Knott right between the eyes. The eyes rolled inward a moment before he fell face forward into his mashed potatoes and gravy.

Instinctively, Ginny Girl reached for him but Fagan's words stopped and froze her. "Ginny Girl, you pass me some more chicken now," he said. "And then we'll go to your bed."

She swallowed hard and said, "Yes sir, Mr. Smith. And then are you takin' me away?"

"You got any money hid in this sorry shack?"

"A few dollars. And there's them horses and pigs and—"

"The money, the horses and *you*," Fagan growled, his big teeth busting the chicken bones as he reached for more whiskey.

When he was finished eating, Fagan belched and

pushed back from the table. "Good chicken," he said.

"Thank you, Mr. Smith."

"Let's go rut in the bed now."

"Yes sir. I . . . I will try to please you if you promise to take me with you when you leave."

"I will do that," Fagan said, thinking it might be nice to have this woman as a traveling companion. And besides, he could always dump her anyplace on the way to Montana. "But I am not one to keep a woman. She has to pay her own way."

"Like I said," Ginny told him, "we have very little money."

"Any jewelry or stuff we could pawn or sell in Cheyenne?"

"A few things. Not much though."

"Well," he said as he began to unbutton his pants. "We'll see how it goes. Come in here and show me what you got."

Ginny paused. "What about Everett? Are we just gonna leave him facedown in his plate?"

"For the present. After we're done, you can dig his grave and bury him while I rest. I don't want him here stinkin' up this hole."

"Are we leavin' right away?"

Fagan had been giving that question a good deal of thought. It was possible that he could ride one of the Knott horses to Cheyenne in time to catch Marshal Custis Long and ambush him before the officer left on westbound Union Pacific. Sure, it was possible. But, on the other hand, what was the hurry? He could stay here a week or two and then go to Montana either alone or with this homesteader's widow woman . . . if she pleased him.

"Not right away," he said. "You're gonna butcher a

hog tomorrow and cook us some ham and pork chops. How much whiskey is in this shack?"

"About four jugs."

Fagan did a quick calculation. "I guess that and the hog will hold us a week or two. You get any visitors?"

"Not much."

"If visitor's come, you go to the door and ask 'em to go away. If they don't, I'll shoot 'em and you'll have to dig more graves. Is that clear?"

"You'd just shoot someone who wanted to visit?"

"I would. You know that I would."

"Yes, sir. I know that."

Fagan went into the bedroom and undressed. When the woman didn't appear, he yelled, "Hurry up and get in here!"

"Yes, sir, Mr. Smith!"

He stared at her in the doorway. "You got any kinfolk in these parts?"

"No."

"Where they at?"

"Arkansas."

"Good," Fagan said. "I'd rather kinfolks was far away. They meddle."

Ginny nodded and said, "You ain't going to hurt me, are you? Mr. Knott, he liked to hurt me sometimes. He'd spank me like I was a little girl. Spank me real hard with his hand and sometimes even with his belt. Then he'd get on me and do it real hard so that I thought I was being split nearly in half."

"You should have shot him yourself," Fagan told her.

"I thought about it a lot, but I didn't have the nerve."

"That's good."

She bent her head a little to one side, surprised by that comment. "Why is it good?"

"Because now I don't have worry about you shooting me," Fagan told her. "Now take that rag off and get over here right now."

She stared at him for a moment, eyes widening. "Why, you're already stiff and big. Bigger than Everett, by a good deal. I fear that you might split me in half too."

"Naw," Fagan said. "Come over here and I'll be gentle with you, Ginny Girl."

She undressed and when she did, Fagan knew that he was going to stay here in this bed for at least the next two weeks while she cooked and serviced his every need and desire. She was a little on the thin side without much fat, like the chicken she had throttled and fried. But Ginny Girl would be good to the bone and he meant to please her and himself so that she would learn what a real man could do when he set his mind to the pleasure of the flesh.

"Oh, Mr. Smith!" she cried when he poled her to the straw mattress. "Oh my goodness!"

She clutched him tight and he told her to wrap her shapely little legs around his waist and act like a wanton woman instead of a poor little homesteader's wife. And when she complied, Fagan laughed hard and got right down to the pleasurable business of satisfying the flesh.

Chapter 11

Longarm was rudely awakened from his afternoon nap by Mrs. Gimshaw when she bumped his feather bed.

"You're going to have to get up so I can change the sheets," she announced without a smile or apology.

Longarm had decided that, while he admired the tough old biddy, he didn't much like her. "All right, Mrs. Grimshaw, just leave the room and I'll get up and get dressed."

"No need to do that," she said, pulling the sheets off his naked body and studying it with a critical eye. "You sure you haven't got any lice down there."

The woman actually pointed at his exposed crotch and Longarm, not accustomed to be eyed critically, snorted, "No."

"Well, you sure are scarred."

"It comes with the profession."

Mabel's eyes narrowed. "Marshal," she asked, "have you ever killed anyone for money?"

"Only the money they stole and wouldn't give back without a fight."

"Humph!" The old woman folded her sizable forearms

across her breast and said, "I'd like to hire me a killer. One that would kill my ex-husband nice and slow."

Longarm was trying to hustle out of the soft bed but he stopped. "You can't do that. It would be murder and you'd either hang or go to prison for life."

"It would be damn well worth it, Marshal. My husband deserves to be shot. I'd do it and take the consequences except that Otto is far better with a gun than I am. In a shoot-out, I'd probably be the one to die of lead poisoning."

Longarm reached for a robe that was resting on a nearby chair. Covering himself, he sat down in the chair and said, "What'd Otto do to you, Mabel?"

"Took up with a younger woman after I bore him six kids and worked like a slave most of my life helping him build up a livery right here in Cheyenne. Now, he's hired some help and he just sits around and enjoys the money I helped make possible for him to earn in his old age. That and he fusses with the younger woman he ain't never got around to marrying."

"He sounds like kind of a rat, all right," Longarm said with sympathy.

"Worse'n a rat! Ten times worse. I thought of poisoning him, but I don't know how I'd get it in his food or liquor. Whenever Otto sees me comin', he runs. I couldn't get within a block of his livery or house without him being suspicious. Otto is worthless, but he ain't stupid and he knows I'd not hesitate to do him in for keeps. I wasted the best years of my life helpin' that rotten scum."

Longarm had heard this story, or versions of it, a hundred times in his law career. Good women being dumped by bad men for younger women. It was an old story and so he just sat there in the chair trying to look sympathetic.

"The thing of it is, Marshal, I was always—"

"Custis. Please call me Custis since we're already so familiar with each other."

"Well, Custis," Mabel continued, "Otto surely deserves to die slow and I don't much care about what happens to me after I kill him . . . as long as he's suffered real bad."

Longarm was beginning to think that Mabel Grimshaw was quite serious about killing her low-down husband. "Look," he said. "Things didn't turn out so bad for you. This is a nice house, and from what I can see, Miss Danner treats you well and I'm sure that you have some good friends."

"Humph! Other than Miss Danner, I haven't got a friend in the world. I'm just a bitter woman that nobody wants to be around. Besides, how'd you like to be old and 'treated well'? How would charity suit you when you've been used up and tossed away?"

"Not well, I guess," Longarm admitted. "But I've seen a lot of hangings and they're not pretty. That's not where you want to end up, Mabel."

"I guess not. What if I killed that double-crossin' Otto in self-defense?"

Longarm's eyes narrowed. "What do you mean by that?"

"Just what I said. He's trying to kill me, but I kill him first?"

"Mabel, you're talking strange. I think you need to reconsider whatever it is that you're planning to do to Mr. Grimshaw."

"I been festerin' and stewin' over this injustice for years, Marshal. So when you came here, I decided to speak right up about this matter and get your own thoughts. Now that I've heard them, it don't change what

I intend to do. But thank you for your honesty."

Longarm was concerned. This woman was filled with hatred and it had poisoned her thinking. Yet, she still seemed a decent enough sort and it was obvious that she'd been wronged. "Mabel, have you spoken to anyone besides me about how much you hate your ex-husband?"

"Miss Danner knows I hate him and so does most everyone else in Cheyenne. Once, when I seen Mr. Grimshaw parading around with his new woman, I grabbed some tomatoes off'a a cart and painted them both!"

She bent and flexed her right bicep. "I have a good arm on me still. I can hit a runnin' rabbit with a rock. Had to when I was growin' up and half starved all the time. Never waste a bullet on a rabbit, my pappy used to say. Hit 'em with a rock or a stick and save the lead."

Longarm watched as the big, angry woman remade his bed. "Mabel," he said when she was collecting the dirty linen, "I sure wish you'd change your mind about killing your ex-husband. Remember that the Lord says, 'Vengeance is mine.' "

"Well, the Lord wasn't married to Otto Grimshaw for forty-three years only to be dumped for a young hussy."

"Maybe," Longarm said, grasping for any words that might help this tortured soul, "Mr. Grimshaw will go to hell when he dies and you'll go to heaven . . . providing, of course . . . that you don't *kill* Mr. Grimshaw."

"If we both go to hell, I'll go with a smile and watch that old bastard burn, whimper and howl. I'm a helluva lot tougher than Otto ever was and I like heat. I've lived in the cold country all of my life and I'm sick of it. Heat would feel good . . . even in hell."

Longarm saw he was getting nowhere. "All right, but I've warned you. And my advice holds that you ought to just bury the hatchet and let bygones be bygones. Water under the bridge, Mabel. That's all it is."

"I'll bury the hatchet handle all the way up his skinny ass! Then I'll pull it out and bury it in his head!"

Longarm was startled by the woman's anger. Not that he wasn't accustomed to seeing bitter women, but Mabel Grimshaw was in a class all by herself.

"Maybe you should talk to a preacher. Might make you see the value of forgiveness."

"Humph! You gonna forgive the man that shot you in the shoulder?"

"No, I'm going to find and arrest him."

"That will be the day! I bet you shoot him dead on sight."

Longarm gave up. "Mabel, thanks for the bed change."

She stopped at the doorway to his bedroom, an arm full of dirty linen clutched to her ample breasts and a heart full of burning hatred. "Thanks for listenin' and tellin' me what will happen when I kill Otto. You even gave me an idea of how to get him where it hurts most before he dies."

This was not good news. "I did?"

"Yes you did, Marshal."

"How is that?"

"Just never you mind. And I'd appreciate it if you didn't tell Miss Danner about our talk. She gets upset easy."

"But—"

"I'm askin' you for your word, Marshal."

"And if I refuse to give it?"

"Might not be too smart. You still got five more days to go in that bed."

Longarm almost shivered because Mrs. Mabel Grimshaw was not a person to be taken lightly. "All right," he agreed. "I won't say anything about our conversation to Miss Danner."

"I'll hold you to your word, Marshal."

When Mabel was gone, Longarm climbed back in his bed and stared at the ceiling. He couldn't quite believe the conversation he'd just had with that big old woman. But it had happened, and he had an uneasy feeling that Otto Grimshaw was not long for this world.

"Somehow, I need to stop it," he said aloud to himself, although he had not the faintest idea of how.

The very next day, Mrs. Grimshaw failed to appear at Allison Danner's house. When Allison came home from the hospital to give Longarm some lunch, he asked about the older woman's absence.

"Oh," Allison said, "she went to visit a friend today."

He felt relieved. "She did? That's fine."

"Yes, I was surprised when she asked for the day off. I didn't even know Mabel had a friend to visit."

Suddenly, Longarm remembered his conversation with Mabel and how she'd declared that she didn't have a "friend in the world."

"Custis, what's wrong? Your expression just changed."

"Mabel doesn't have a friend to visit."

"But—"

Longarm was already getting out of bed. "Do you know where we can find her?"

"You can't get out of that bed and go running around. Custis, what's wrong with you!"

"Missus Grimshaw is going to kill Mr. Grimshaw today," Longarm said without the slightest doubt. "And we've got to stop her."

"I don't understand!"

"I'll explain later. Help me get dressed. We've got to find her before she commits murder."

Five minutes later, Longarm and Allison Danner were rushing up the street with Longarm shouting, "Where is Mr. Grimshaw's livery?"

"It's over on 5th Street."

"How far?"

"Two long blocks. Custis, you shouldn't be doing anything so strenuous! Why are we going to Mr. Grimshaw's Livery?"

"I think you can guess the answer."

"Oh my heavens!" Allison cried. "Do you really think that that Mrs. Grimshaw would actually kill him?"

"I'm sure of it," Longarm said, hurrying along the street.

When they reached the Grimshaw Stable, there wasn't a person in sight. Just lots of for-sale horses milling in a big round pen. But then, just as they were trying to decide what to do, Longarm heard a horrific scream come from inside the barn. An instant later, a pale woman of about forty ran out of the barn with her eyes filled with terror.

"Hold it!" Longarm shouted. "What's going on in there?"

"Mabel has Otto tied down and she's cutting the life out of him with a knife!"

Allison paled and Longarm drew his six-gun with his left hand and raced into the barn. He could hear a desperate struggle and loud, tortured breathing coming from somewhere in the rear of the dimly lit barn.

"Mabel!" Allison cried. "Mabel!"

"Help! Help!" a weak voice pleaded. "She's killin' me! I'm bleeding to death!"

Longarm moved back toward the rear of the barn. Horses, spooked by the smell of fresh blood, were stamping and snorting in their individual stalls. One big gray horse was tearing his stall apart because he was so frightened. "Mabel," Longarm said. "Come out with your hands up."

"You're going to have to shoot me!" the woman hollered. " 'Cause I just done in this miserable, lecherous old man."

Longarm rushed forward, and as his eyes adjusted, the outline of the pair emerged. It wasn't a pretty sight. Mabel had somehow stunned her former husband and then tied him spread-eagled in an empty stall. She had then pulled down the old man's pants and crudely gelded him.

"Stand back, Marshal," Mabel warned placing the knife to Otto's throat. "I took what mattered to him most and now I'm going to cut his neck like the pig he is with this dull and rusty old skinnin' knife."

"Mabel," Longarm pleaded, as the big woman knelt over the semi-conscious man. "Stop it! You've done enough to Otto. You don't need to kill him and be hanged or sent to prison for the last days of your life."

Otto Grimshaw began to cry and then sob hysterically. "I'm a dead man. I'm a dead man!" he repeated. "No good for no young women anymore. Look what she done to me!"

Longarm took a few steps closer to the barn. "Mabel," he said softly. "Don't cut his throat. If Otto doesn't bleed to death, he'll suffer far more than if he were dead."

For a long moment, Mabel hovered in a crouch over the writhing, sobbing old man and then she dropped her knife in the bloody straw bedding. "Marshal," she hissed, "I hate to admit it, but you're right. He's ruined now. He won't even be able to piss a straight stream. Instead, he'll just squirt like a little baby and wet his damned old self. It'll shame Otto every last day of his miserable life."

Beside him, Longarm heard a thump and turned around to see Allison Danner lying on the barn floor passed out cold.

"Marshal, you shouldn't have let her come. Miss Danner is a lady."

"Yeah," Longarm said. "Now get away from Otto and let me try to stop that bleeding while you go find a doctor."

"Me?"

"Sure," Longarm said, brushing past the woman. "If you do that, a jury will go easier on you for that knife work."

Mabel nodded with understanding. But when she left the barn, she made no effort whatsoever to hide the blood on her dress and she sure as blue blazes didn't hurry to find a doctor either.

Chapter 12

Fagan and Ginny were an odd pair as they rode two ugly sorrel plow horses into Cheyenne leading a milk cow on a tether and herding two noisy pigs. Heads turned to stare, but when Fagan stared back, men dropped their eyes and looked away because the big, black-bearded man was so physically imposing.

"Fagan," she asked, unable to keep the question inside any longer, "what are we going to do here in Cheyenne?"

"Sell the pigs and these plow horses for starters. Then get us a room, get drunk and screw a few days."

"We already done a whole lot of that at the farm."

"More won't hurt either of us," Fagan said, embarrassed by the snorting pigs that had chased a dog that had dared to challenge them. The dog, tail tucked under its legs, had disappeared in an alley with the pigs close on his heels.

"Damn them pigs! We'd better go after 'em."

"They always did hate dogs. They'll knock over small ones and eat 'em while they're still down and kickin'."

"Let's get those pigs sold right away. Ought to be

worth a few dollars. What do you think these ugly old horses are worth?"

"They're only about ten and still strong. One of the best pullin' teams in our part of the county. I'd say that they ought to fetch fifty dollars for the pair."

"Good," Fagan said as he reined the plow horse up an alley where he could hear the dog yelping as if it were being slaughtered.

When they came upon the pigs, there was blood on their snouts but the dog was nowhere to be found. Ginny shrugged. "Looks like this one got clean away but I'll bet the pigs killed him anyways. That dog probably crawled under a building to die."

"Where can we sell the damned pigs before they kill any more dogs?"

"Butcher shop just up the street will buy 'em."

"Then get a rope around their ugly heads and lead them over to the butcher shop while I find a livery and get these horses sold."

"Grimshaw's Livery is around the corner on 5th Street. He buys all kinds of horses."

Fagan nodded and gave Ginny a shove to hurry her off the horse. She fell hard and whimpered. "You didn't have to do that, Fagan!"

"Rope the pigs and meet me at Grimshaw's," he ordered, heading back to the main street.

But when he got to the livery, it was locked up tight. A shoeless boy with freckles and red hair was sitting by the barn doing nothing at all. Fagan dismounted. "Boy?"

"Yes, sir?"

"Where's the owner of this livery?"

The boy sized up the big man. "You want me to water or tend to them big farm horses, mister?"

"I asked you a question and I expect a fast answer."

The boy jumped to his feet. "Mr. Grimshaw is in a real bad way. He got his balls cut off with a rusty old butcher knife."

Fagan was not a man greatly interested in the fate of other men, but this response did grab his attention. "Come again?"

The boy repeated his statement and this time he added, "His old ex-wife Mrs. Grimshaw did it. And she'd have cut his throat, too, 'cept Marshal Custis Long rushed into the barn and put a stop to it."

"*Who* put a stop to it?"

"Marshal Long. Why, he's from Denver and he's got a wounded shoulder but he put a stop to it or else Mr. Grimshaw would be a goner. Might be still. Doctor says he's in bad shape and don't want to live anymore."

Fagan felt a stillness come over him. "What does this marshal look like?"

When the boy had given a good description, Fagan knew there could be no mistake about it being Custis Long from Denver. "Boy, where is this marshal staying?"

The boy was beginning to lose his fear of the huge, imposing man. "You ask a lot of questions, mister. Might be worth at least a nickel, I'd think."

"Might be." Fagan would have grabbed the kid and shaken him half to death, but he didn't want to take the chance that the boy escaped. Better, he decided, to pay the nickel for this extremely valuable bit of information.

"Here," he said, tossing a coin into the dirt at the boy's feet. "Now where is this marshal staying?"

"You a friend of his?"

"I'm the one asking the questions."

"Yes, sir. He's recovering over at Miss Danner's house."

"And where would that be?"

The boy gave Fagan directions and then said, "You want to know anything more, mister?"

"Is the marshal hurt much?"

"Right shoulder is bad. Can't use his gun with that hand. I'd say he's in bad shape, but Miss Danner is pretty and I guess that big marshal ain't in no hurry to leave her house." The boy actually winked. "Could be he's getting more than a good bandaging, if you know what I mean."

Fagan smiled. "Yeah. I know what you mean. I got these two horses to sell. Who else in Cheyenne will buy 'em?"

"Might try the Acme Stable just two blocks up the street. Want me to introduce you to the owner? Only cost you twenty-five cents. And I could maybe help you get a good price for them ugly plow horses."

"Now how the hell would you do that?"

"Man who owns Acme is my uncle."

Fagan actually liked this enterprising kid. Reminded him of himself at that age . . . always looking for a chance to make pocket money.

"All right. If I sell the horses to your uncle for a good price, I'll give you the money."

"Come along then," the boy said, hitching up his baggy and patched pants and shuffling his bare feet through the dust.

Fagan got his fifty dollars for the two horses, but he had to throw in the poor saddles, blankets and bridles. He took the money and went back to Grimshaw's where Ginny was waiting.

"How'd you do?"

"I got the fifty dollars. Did you sell the pigs?"

"Yes."

"Give me the money."

Ginny took a back step. "They were *my* horses and *my* pigs. I reckon I ought to have some of that money for myself."

Fagan advanced. "Give me the damn pig money or I'll break your damned jaw!"

Ginny shook and when she saw three men who had overheard Fagan's threat looking at them with concern, she said, "I guess I'll keep the pig money and find my own way in Cheyenne."

Fagan exploded with anger. He leapt at Ginny, but she was far faster afoot and dashed up the road, old dress flying.

"To hell with her!" Fagan swore.

"Mister," one of the three men said as he walked up, "we heard you threaten that little woman. A man shouldn't do that to a lady."

"She ain't no lady," Fagan said, sizing up the three. "She's just a dirt-poor slut."

The three men colored and when the largest of them clenched his fists, Fagan hit the man in the nose so hard it broke. The man dropped to his knees and Fagan kicked him in the ribs and he collapsed. The other pair attacked, but Fagan grabbed one of them in a headlock and bashed his skull into the barn. The third man did get in a solid lick, but Fagan kicked him in the crotch then hit him three times in the face until he wailed and begged for mercy.

Fagan's blood was up and he was grinning. "Is that the best you three can do?" he challenged. "Why, you boys hardly made me sweat. Next time, you mind your own damn business about how I talk to a woman or a man. Do you understand me?"

The one whose skull he'd slammed into the barn was unconscious and couldn't answer. The other pair, however, were conscious and thoroughly whipped.

"Yes sir!" one of them gulped. "We don't want no more trouble."

"That's right," the other said, holding his broken and bloodied nose. "No more trouble."

Fagan spat on them and then headed up the street. He'd have liked to have had the damned pig money but at least he had the fifty dollars. As for Ginny Girl, she could do whatever she pleased. Most likely, she'd become just another town whore.

The main thing on Fagan's mind was finding and killing Marshal Custis Long.

Chapter 13

Longarm looked up from his bed to see Allison standing in the doorway with a brimming glass of brandy in her hand. Her eyes were red from crying and she looked very sad.

"What's wrong?" he asked, quite sure that he already knew the answer.

"It's Mabel. Tomorrow is her sentencing and I'm afraid that judge will send her to prison for what she did to Mr. Grimshaw."

Longarm shared the same fear. "At least Grimshaw didn't die like we thought he might for the first day or two. If he had, I'm afraid that Mabel would never have another day of freedom and she might even have been sentenced to hang."

"But she'll still go to prison, won't she?"

Longarm would have liked to have said no, but that wouldn't have been the truth so he said, "I expect so. What Mabel did was damned serious."

Allison came on into the room and Longarm could see that this wasn't her first glass of brandy. She sat down on his bed and tried to smile and failed. "Custis," she began, "I knew how much Mabel hated her ex-husband and I'd often heard her threaten to do him in, but I never really took her words seriously. It's clear now that I made a big mistake."

"She's poisoned with hatred," Longarm said, "but can you really blame the woman? After all, she probably did work like a dog for all those years to build up that livery into the business it is today."

"Oh, she did!" Allison said, offering Longarm brandy, which was really in a full water tumbler rather than a smaller whiskey glass. "I've heard people tell me that it was Mabel, not Otto, who did all the work. That she was the one who would be out in all kinds of snow and sleet, mucking out the pens, feeding the stock and nursing them back to health when they were ill. I'm told that Otto Grimshaw is about as lazy as a man can be."

"Well," Longarm said, taking a big swallow of the brandy and feeling it go down warm all the way to the bottom of his belly, "there you have it. Mabel does all the work, but her no count husband winds up with all the money . . . and a much younger woman."

"It's unjust!" Allison said, her eyes shiny with tears and outrage. "Can't you put in a good word with the judge for her?"

"I don't even know the man."

"His name is Judge Wilfred Pettigrew."

"I never heard of him."

"He is an old bachelor and he lives at the Cheyenne House right downtown. He likes his cigars and whiskey. I think he was a colonel in the Confederacy and is from West Virginia. Aren't you from the South?"

"As a matter of fact, I am," Longarm said. "And I was also born and raised in West Virginia."

"There you are!" Allison shouted. "You and Wilfred will hit it off like a couple of long lost brothers. Were you in the Confederate army?"

"I don't like to talk about it."

"That's all right. Just tell him you were and he'll be eating out of your hand. And the fact that you're also from West Virginia is perfect! I'm sure that the judge will like you."

"That may or may not be the case," Longarm said, "but I doubt that it would make any difference in his sentencing of Mabel."

"But it might. Please, would you go over there and ask to talk to the man? I know that you're supposed to stay in bed but . . ."

"I'm sick and tired of staying in bed," Longarm snorted. "And I will go see this Judge Pettigrew. I'm sure that it won't hurt to explain to him how shabbily Mabel was treated by her ex-husband and how that brought her to the act of temporary madness leading to Otto's castration."

Allison shuddered. "I almost feel sorry for Otto. Castration must render a man more than physically impotent. It must also have a profound and lasting effect on his mind."

"I'm sure it does."

Allison took another drink. "I know that Otto is old, but he did have that younger woman and I've no doubt that he was . . . well, capable of . . . of sex."

"No doubt," Longarm said, seeing color rise in Allison's cheeks.

"Custis, I don't want to pry, but have you ever . . . oh," she giggled, "this is rather embarrassing."

"Have I what?"

"Have you ever been impotent? I mean, even for one night?"

It was Longarm's turn to blush. "No."

"But you can imagine what it would be like, can't you?"

"Not really."

She looked closely at him. "I suppose you couldn't. I mean, you just *ooze* masculinity. I feel it every time I enter this room and we're alone."

"You do?"

"Oh, yes. You're an animal, Custis. A big, wounded but still powerful animal. That's how I think of you."

Longarm was amused. "Am I any particular kind of animal?"

"Certainly." Allison drank more brandy and gave him a loose but wide and inviting smile. "You're a tawny mountain lion . . . a long, muscular cougar. And you know what else?"

"No."

"I'm a lamb. And I fantasize in my daydreams that you jump on me and then you . . . you eat me."

Longarm was flabbergasted. "Why that's the craziest thing I've ever heard from a pretty young woman. Why would I want to eat someone like you?"

"Because I'm good to eat, I guess." Allison giggled, winked provocatively and then handed Longarm the glass of excellent brandy. "And you're right, it is crazy to have such a wicked and perverse fantasy, but there you have it and I can't help it."

Longarm took another deep swallow of the liquor,

placed the glass on the nightstand and reached for the woman. "Would you like to be pounced on, Allie? And then eaten by me right now?"

She swallowed hard and licked her lips. "Oh my goodness *yes!*"

That was all that Longarm needed to know. Even with his bad shoulder, he had no trouble helping the pretty young woman undress and then he pounced on her like the cougar in her titillating fantasy. Longarm had the feeling that Allison wanted to be ravished . . . completely and with a small degree of savagery.

So he did his best despite the pain in his shoulder. He took Allison hard and ravished her from top to bottom until she was screaming with delight mixed with a tiny dose of fear. Longarm used her as a stallion would a mare, a dog would a bitch in heat and she loved him for it. And when he'd satisfied and left her gasping and sweaty, he finally took his own lustful pleasure and then he climbed out of the bed.

"Oh good heavens," she whispered, grabbing the glass and offering him a toast. "Marshal Long, I am your sex slave forever!"

He laughed. "I thought I'd given you enough hard rutting to last at least a week."

"I've gone without it too long. And now, I'm just a little drunk and well satisfied but eager for more at the first crack I get at you."

Longarm was flattered but firm. "Tomorrow morning you're going to have a hell of a rotten hangover, if you don't stop drinking that stuff."

"I don't care about tomorrow morning. I fear that it's going to be a bad, bad day for our poor old Mabel."

"I'm going over to see Judge Pettigrew right now."

"Thank you, Custis. Mabel Grimshaw doesn't deserve to spend her last days locked up in some smelly cell. She's got a big heart."

"Yeah, but her big heart is corroded with hatred."

"Not anymore, I'll bet. Mabel got her revenge and I'm sure that she's feeling much better now. Maybe the act of castrating Otto Grimshaw has cleansed her heart of hatred."

"I really doubt that," Longarm said. "How about a little help buttoning up my shirt?"

"Of course."

Longarm had to struggle to disengage himself from Allison because she was quite drunk and wanting more action. But he had made up his mind to talk to the judge and so he headed for the door.

"Come back soon, big boy!" Allison said, kicking up one bare leg and then tumbling to the floor in a giggling heap in front of her door.

"Close that door then brew some strong black coffee," he advised, "or you'll feel like death tomorrow."

As he went out the door, Longarm shifted his Colt revolver around to his right hip, butt forward so that he could reach for the weapon with his good left arm and hand. Before he got to the street, he stood in Allison's front yard and practiced a few left handed draws and although it was awkward, it worked. He was slower with the left hand and he wasn't going to have his usual accuracy, but he was still better than most men with a pistol.

Longarm headed for the Cheyenne House. Allison, although drunk, was right. Perhaps by talking to the southern-born judge, buying him a drink and a good cigar, he could help Mabel out and get a more lenient sentence.

He had liked the old biddy despite her hardness and,

right now, she needed a break. As he walked up the street, the sun was setting and it was directly in his eyes. Longarm tipped the flat brim of his brown hat a little lower to shade his eyes from the sun.

He didn't see Fagan watching him leave Allison Danner's house. Fagan was hiding behind some tall bushes. There was gun in his hand, but the sun was also directly in his eyes when he tried to take aim on Longarm's back.

Failing that, he allowed Longarm to continue up the street. He'd seen the tall lawman from Denver fumble practicing his left-handed draw. Fagan was now very confident that, when Longarm returned from his nightly jaunt, he would be easy pickings inside the Danner house.

And besides, he'd heard the laughter of a drunken female and caught the briefest glimpse of a naked woman in the house and that was certainly worth investigating.

Chapter 14

Allison Danner was brewing a fresh cup of black coffee and humming a happy tune when she turned and saw Fagan standing in her kitchen's doorway. She was sober enough to let out a cry of alarm a moment before Fagan rushed across the kitchen and clamped his hand over her mouth.

Grabbing a kitchen knife with his free hand, Fagan placed it to Allison's throat and hissed, "If you scream again, I'll cut you from ear to ear."

Allison froze in terror.

"Where's Marshal Long going?"

She was too rattled to lie so she blurted the truth. "To see Judge Pettigrew."

"What for?"

"He's trying to help a friend get a lighter sentence."

Fagan didn't care about any of that. He turned the naked woman around and studied the fear in her eyes. "How long will Custis Long be gone?"

"I . . . I don't know. Maybe not very long."

"Long enough for what I've got in mind," Fagan said,

dragging Allison out of the kitchen and into her bedroom. He slapped her hard and threw her onto the bed.

"I'm going to have my pleasure with you, girl. And, if you so much as let out a peep, I'll kill you in your own bed. Understand?"

Allison understood and knew there was nothing she could do but submit or be murdered. But when Longarm returned, she would need to be ready to help him in any way possible or both of them would soon be dead meat.

Longarm and Judge Pettigrew had hit it off from the start. They'd talked about the South and the terrible consequences it now faced in the aftermath of the Civil War. Both Custis and the judge were men who had fought for their beliefs and, when the battles had all been won and lost, they'd decided to go to the West rather than deal with the carpetbaggers and the years of heartache associated with Reconstruction.

"The South may yet rise again," Judge Pettigrew swore. "But, if she does, it will be long after you and I are dead and buried. What a terrible price she paid during that war."

"The whole country paid a price," Longarm told him. "But out here on the western frontier, the scars aren't very deep and people seemed inclined to forgive and forget."

"That's because the West was spared the awful sacrifices and carnage."

Longarm and the judge were sipping good southern whiskey. Now, Longarm got around to the subject that had brought him to the Cheyenne House. "I've come to ask you to be lenient tomorrow when you sentence Mrs. Mabel Grimshaw for the assault she committed on her ex-husband."

The judge, a portly man whose eyes reflected a keen intelligence, steepled his stubby fingers and asked, "And why should I do that? The damage she did to Otto Grimshaw was severe and delivered with considerable malice."

"This is true," Longarm agreed. "But given the circumstances leading up to the attack, I think that Mabel deserves to be let off with only a warning."

"A warning? Marshal, surely you jest! She almost killed Otto and one can hardly imagine the years of mental anguish she has inflicted on what remains of that man."

"Just as Otto inflicted on Mabel. Judge, I'm sure that you are aware that Otto tossed his wife aside after she had worked like a slave to build his livery business. And did she get any compensation for all those years of hard work and loyalty? No, she did not. She was wronged and left to fend for herself in poverty. Even worse, Otto flaunted his new young female conquests!"

"Yes," Pettigrew admitted, "he did that. Otto is not much of a gentleman. I have no respect for him whatsoever and what he did to Mabel was wrong. However—"

"The man got exactly what he deserved!" Longarm exclaimed. "Judge, we are southerners who understand that ladies are never treated so shabbily. And Mabel was, until this last incident, a good, honest and respected lady."

"That's true. A diamond in the rough."

"If you simply scold Mabel and warn her that, should she ever revert to such violence again, she will be sent to prison, I think then you could let her go free and know that justice was well served in Cheyenne."

The judge frowned. "If I did that, there will be men in this town who will want to nail my hide to the barn wall."

"And there will be women in this town who will consider you a crusader for the fairer sex and a great and courageous man."

"Ah, yes," the judge mused, "that is also true."

"Then you'll do it? You'll not send Mrs. Grimshaw to prison?"

"No," the judge said, "I will not. And since she has no assets, I will not even require her to make monetary compensation to Otto."

"Thank you," Longarm said. "It is the right and fair thing to do."

Pettigrew reached for the bottle. "I think we should have a toast to ladies and to poor Mrs. Grimshaw."

Longarm thought that a fine idea and, after several more toasts, he got up to leave and return to Allison Danner's house. He knew that the judge's decision would greatly improve her low spirits.

The lights were out at Miss Danner's house when he opened her front gate and moved up to her door. That was good, Longarm thought, because it meant Allison had probably gone to bed to sleep off the liquor.

Longarm eased the door open and paused to let his eyes adjust to the darkness in the house and that's when he smelled the faint, unfamiliar odor of cigarette smoke.

Did Allison ever smoke cigarettes?

Longarm knew she did not so he backed out of the house and gave the troubling matter some thought. The tobacco was not his own brand, of that he was certain. Then who had entered this house during the hour or so he had been absent?

Longarm could not come up with an answer.

"Allison?" he whispered, edging his gun out of his holster with his left hand and cocking back the hammer as

116

he ducked low and entered the house. "Allison? Are you alone?"

Now he saw a faint crack of lamp light under her bedroom door and that told him she was still awake. But the smell of cigarette smoke was now stronger in his nostrils and he had the feeling that it came from the bedroom.

"Allison?" he said, louder this time.

Suddenly, the door burst open and Fagan filled the space of light. Longarm and the killer fired at the same time but Longarm's feet were planted solidly on the floor while Fagan was in motion.

Longarm felt as if he were firing in slow motion. As if he were struggling to pull the trigger as the gun bucked in his left hand. The range between them was right, not more than ten feet and with the smoke and din, he was not sure if he were hitting Fagan with good body shots. It was only when the outlaw's gun tipped downward and emptied three bullets into the floor that Longarm knew he had mortally wounded his man.

Fagan cursed on his way down and he was still trying to pull the trigger of his pistol when Longarm shot him through the top of his head spattering blood and bits of brain and bone back into the bedroom.

"Custis!" Allison cried.

Longarm hurried to the woman who was still naked and ravaged. Her face was bruised, her lips swollen and one eye blacked from a punch.

He cradled Allison in his arms while she wept her bitter tears. Only later did he dress the woman and lead her out of the bloody room and take her to a friend and a neighbor.

"Allison needs your help," he told the woman who had

appeared at the door. "She's been through something pretty rough."

The neighbor was in her forties and immediately revealed her kind nature when she hugged Allison Danner and hurried her inside saying, "You'll be all right. Everything will be all right."

Longarm turned on the porch and saw that there were a number of people standing out by the street. No doubt they'd heard the thunder of rapid gunshots and were wondering what in the world had happened.

"My name is Deputy United States Marshal Custis Long," he told them in a loud voice that hardened with authority. "There's been a shooting, but it is none of your concern. Everyone go back to your houses."

"Who got shot?" a man in a bathroom robe and slippers asked.

"A killer," Longarm said.

"Where is he?"

Longarm didn't want to tie the shooting to Allison, but he knew that it was not a thing he could keep people from knowing. So he told them and then again ordered everyone to clear the street and go home.

"And the next person who asks me a question will be arrested and taken to jail," he said.

That seemed to do the trick. The people turned and headed back to their houses. Longarm went to find a mortician and then he thought he'd go back to the Cheyenne House and have another drink with his new friend, Judge Pettigrew.

Chapter 15

There was a lot of fussing and waiting the next morning while the local marshal, who had been away on vacation, rushed back to Cheyenne, clearly vexed that a killing had taken place in his town during his absence. His name was Skeeter Hopkins and he was a pompous man who waxed the tips of his handlebar mustache and smelled of cheap cologne.

"I don't care if you are a United States Marshal; you should have gone to my office and informed my deputies of what was going on!" Hopkins thundered.

Longarm was in no mood for diplomacy. "Marshal," he said, "the man I killed had already murdered someone in Denver and has probably killed quite a few others. I acted in self-defense and to save Miss Danner from additional harm."

"That's right," the shaken woman said. "If Custis . . . I mean, Marshal Long, had not arrived just in the nick of time who can say what that horrible beast would have done besides the beating I'd already received."

Skeeter Hopkins blushed. "I guess that's true enough," he admitted.

Longarm and Allison had agreed that no good would come of her admission that she had been raped by Fagan. As it was, things were difficult enough.

The marshal turned away from Allison to study Longarm's bandaged shoulder. "Did you get shot last night at Miss Danner's house?"

"No," Longarm replied. "But the same man I killed had already wounded me on the train up from Denver. Dr. Lane bandaged me up and said I'd be fit a few weeks."

"Well," Marshal Hopkins said, "you feds ought to let us local people know what in the hell is going on when you arrive. But you never do. You just come into our towns and act like you're above the local law your damn selves!"

Longarm had heard enough. "Skeeter, if you'll excuse us," he grated, "we've got things to take care of."

"Wait a minute!"Hopkins challenged. "How long are you going to be in my town?"

Longarm said, "You have my word that I'll be on the next train out of Cheyenne."

"Good!"

Longarm was too angry to risk a reply so he left the officer and headed for the train station. Allison Danner tried to keep up with him. "Custis, what are you going to do when you reach Helena?"

"I'm going to see if I can prevent any more of Jed King's children from being murdered for a stolen bounty that I doubt even exists."

They were almost to the train station when someone came running up from behind. "Excuse me, Marshal Long. Could I talk to you a moment?"

Longarm turned to see a small but attractive young woman hurrying up the street. She was poorly dressed, but her hair was combed and her face was scrubbed clean. There were some old bruises on her face that had gone from purple to a yellowish cast yet her eyes were clear and a deep blue.

"I'm Mrs. Everett Knott," she said by way of introduction, eyes darting back and forth between Longarm and Allison. "Marshal, could I talk to you *alone*?"

"Is it important?" Longarm asked. "I'm about to catch a train."

"It won't take long, and yes, it is very important."

Longarm decided that he had a few minutes to spare. "Allison, would you excuse us?"

Allison wasn't happy about being asked to leave, but she did.

"Now, Mrs. Knott," Longarm began when they were alone, "what do you want to say to me?"

The homesteader's wife told Longarm in a rush how Fagan had murdered her farmer husband, Everett at their homestead south of Cheyenne. "He made me bury Everett and we stayed at the farm for a week or so. Then we came to Cheyenne and he sold my husband's horses . . . they were a good draft pair worth fifty dollars, but he kept the money for himself."

"Is that a fact," Longarm said, still not sure where this conversation was heading.

"It *is* a fact, Marshal. I sold my two butcher hogs right here in town, but they weren't worth all that much. I only got seven dollars each for 'em and I already had to spend that money for a hotel room and food."

"What has this got to do with me, Mrs. Knott?"

She looked him square in the eye and Longarm saw

121

there was steel in her spine. "Marshal Long, first off I wanted to thank you for killing the man that murdered my husband."

"You are very welcome. Fagan deserved to die."

"He sure as hell did. But what I wanted most to say to you is that everything here in Cheyenne is awful expensive. I haven't been able to find respectable work. Not even washin' clothes or cleanin' rooms. I'm almost out of money and growing more worried by the day."

Longarm figured she wanted a small donation and was about to reach for his wallet but her words stopped him.

"So, Marshal Long, I'm asking you to help me get the fifty dollars that Fagan stole from me when he sold our horses. It would be enough so that I could buy a train ticket back to my folks in Iowa. They'll see to it that I never starve or have to do the wrong things to survive."

"Mrs. Knott, have you talked to the local marshal and his deputies about escorting you up to Fagan's hotel room?"

"No, because everyone has told me that Skeeter Hopkins and his deputy are crooks. If Fagan has my money, they'd find and keep it for themselves. So that's why I'm asking you to help me get the horse money that is rightfully mine."

"I really do have to catch a train to Helena, Montana," Longarm told her as he glanced toward the station. "I'm sorry, but I don't have the time to help you."

Longarm started to leave but the woman caught his sleeve. "Did Fagan have any money on his person when you killed him?"

"No," Longarm replied, "he didn't."

"Then my horse money just *has* to be in his hotel room. He's staying at the Antelope Hotel. Room #8. Couldn't you just take a few minutes and go there with me to find my money?"

Longarm saw that her pretty blue eyes were filling with tears. "Marshal, if you don't help me, I'm afraid of what I might have to do when the rest of my hog money is gone. Sir, you are looking at a desperate woman in need of a gentleman's help! And you are a gentleman, aren't you?"

Longarm was no saint but he'd always been taught to help a lady in distress and she must have guessed that he was a true southern gentleman at heart.

"Listen, Mrs. Knott, I'd really like to help but the train I'm catching leaves soon and I can't afford to miss it."

"But it doesn't pull out for more'n an hour and it'll only take you a few minutes to help me get into Fagan's room."

"Why don't you just go to the room yourself?"

"I tried that, but the hotel clerk told me to get lost. Marshal, I haven't got but a couple dollars to my name. There's only one way I can survive in Cheyenne without money and I don't want to take that downhill road to hell and damnation. Do you understand what I mean?"

Longarm knew exactly what the woman meant—prostitution.

"All right," he reluctantly agreed. "The Antelope Hotel is only a block up the street. I'll help you get into Fagan's room, but Hopkins and his deputy will be plenty steamed if they find out. As it is they feel that I've way overstepped my bounds in Cheyenne."

"What do you care? You're leavin' town and so am I."

"That's one way to look at it, I guess."

Ginny reached up and gave Longarm a kiss on the cheek. "Thank you!"

Longarm said good-bye to Allison and, five minutes later, he was browbeating the desk clerk into giving him the key to room #8. When they went to the little hotel room and opened it up, Longarm smelled the same cigarette smoke that had probably saved his life when he'd gone back to the Danner house last night.

"This room is a pigpen," Longarm said, noting how Fagan had just thrown his filthy clothing on the floor along with remnants of food, crushed cigarettes and empty whiskey bottles.

"He was a brute and a devil," Ginny said, eyes darting from place to place as she tried to decide where to start her search. "But I'm almost sure that Fagan didn't spend all of my plow horse money."

Ginny began by searching Fagan's haversack and saddlebags.

"If you find any letters or papers, give them to me," Longarm told the woman as he lit a cigar and took a seat to see what the desperate widow might turn up.

"Money!" Ginny cried as she opened the saddlebags. "Look, Marshal Long, I just discovered a whole wad of money!"

Longarm jumped out of his chair, suddenly very interested. "Give it to me and I'll count you out your fifty."

"A hundred is fairer," Ginny said, clutching the cash to her bosom, " 'cause of what Fagan took at the farm and what he did to me. I fed him and . . . well, he took whatever he wanted after killing my poor, sweet husband."

"Let me have the cash," Longarm ordered.

Ginny shot a glance at the door but decided she could not bolt past the lawman so she handed the money over

124

to him saying, "Half of that should be mine, sir."

Longarm counted the cash and there was almost four hundred dollars. It was enough to give this destitute homesteader's widow two hundred and use the rest to cover his travel expenses to Helena.

"Here," he said, giving Ginny half of Fagan's stash.

Her hand flew out and snatched the bills away. Ginny looked at some of Fagan's other belongings and said, "Marshal Long, there's probably other things worth money right here in this little hotel room. You gonna keep them for yourself or can I have 'em? If I'm going home to Iowa, I'd rather not arrive in rags like a street beggar. A woman has her pride, you know."

"Keep anything else you find valuable for yourself, Mrs. Knott," Longarm told her, feeling generous. "Is there any correspondence or written material in those saddlebags?"

She shuffled through the pile. "Yes, two letters."

Longarm extended his hand, hoping that the letters would finally give him a clue as to Fagan's background and circumstances relating to the King family.

Unfortunately, the first letter was no help. It was just some impersonal correspondence that Fagan had regarding a pistol he had left at a gunsmith's shop in Denver. But the second letter, although unsigned, was posted from Helena and told Longarm that Fagan had been sent to Denver specifically to find Chester King and *do whatever is necessary to find out where that money is hidden on the King Ranch. Chester must know where it is but we'll keep up the pressure at this end and do whatever it takes to get the answers we need to find that money.*

"Does the letter help you, Marshal Long?"

"It does," Longarm answered. "But I sure wish it was signed so I knew who wrote it back in Helena. If I did, I'd save myself and quite a few others a good deal of grief."

Ginny had found a good pocket knife, several silver dollars and a brass money clip with a few more greenbacks. She looked very pleased as she held up a pair of tooled leather saddlebags, announcing, "These are well made and ought to bring me at least ten dollars."

"Good," Longarm told her. "Now you have plenty of money to return to your hometown in Iowa."

"Yeah, I guess I probably do . . . if I decide that's the place I should go."

"What does that mean?"

"Well," Ginny hedged, shrugging her shoulders and then tossing a few strands of blond hair from her eyes. "My pa beat me and Ma every chance he had. That's why I eloped in the first place. So unless Pa's up and done everyone in the family a favor and died, maybe I shouldn't return."

"How old were you when you eloped?" Longarm asked.

"Almost fifteen."

"You were just a kid."

"I was a woman," Ginny insisted. "But I was livin' in fear all the time. My pa would whip me with a big old razor strop and he nearly killed me a time or two."

"You're older now and maybe you can stand up to him," Longarm said. "And stand up for your mother as well."

"I'd like to do that," Ginny told him. "I'd like to help her out. I can't stand men beatin' on us women all the time. Why do they do that, Marshal? Why?"

"Not all men beat women," he said. "In fact, most don't. You and your mother were unlucky."

"Everett, that's my last husband that Fagan murdered, he never beat me. But he worked me like a mule. Sunup to sundown. I'm only twenty-two, Marshal, but I knew that I'd be an old woman if I kept that up for a few more years."

"Find a man who doesn't make his living farming," Longarm advised. "Find a man who goes to church and takes pride in his profession."

"Do you go to church?"

"Not much anymore," Longarm said, uncomfortable with the subject. "When you hunt and kill men, you sort of . . . well, never mind, Mrs. Knott."

She cocked her head to the side and even the old bruises and her poor clothes couldn't hide the fact that she was still a beauty. "Marshal?"

"Yeah?"

"I wish we were going to Iowa together. I would be proud to introduce you to my family."

"Thank you."

"And I will try to help Momma. I thought about that a lot right after I left Iowa. But then I got to thinking that Ma wouldn't know what to do without Pa and that, bad as things were, she'd be lost and alone if she couldn't live on our family farm."

"Are there any towns near the farm?"

"Oh sure. A couple of nice little towns."

"Then she'd do fine," Longarm assured her. "Do you have any brothers or sisters?"

"Seven of 'em. And they're probably still around those parts. Ain't any of us kids were ever lazy."

"Then that's where you belong," Longarm told her.

"You need a family around you now that your husband is dead."

"Everett wasn't much better than my Pa," Ginny confessed. "Maybe pickin' bad men just naturally runs in my Scottish blood."

"Hogwash! Take your money and return to where you were raised. You've got over two hundred dollars, think about how to use it to your best advantage. You're a lovely young woman and you'll have no trouble at all finding another husband."

Hope sprang to her eyes. "Do you really think I could?"

Longarm nodded. "I'm almost sure of it, Mrs. Knott."

"Virginia," she said, chin lifting with determination. "No more Ginny Girl for me. No sir! I'm gonna go back to my maiden name. So now I'm Miss Virginia Ann Macklin. That's what I was before I came to the West."

"Miss Virginia Ann Macklin is a fine name," Longarm said. "It sounds like the name of a lady."

"Oh," she told him with a wink of her eye, "I'm no lady anymore. But no one knows that except you and me and the dead. And you know what?"

"What?" Longarm asked, hearing the train whistle blow and starting for the door.

"When I get back to Iowa, I'm going to tell everyone that I was married to a tall, handsome United States marshal like you, but that he got shot saving my life and then we spent all our money on doctors and medicine before he finally up and died. That'll get them feelin' sympathetic and they'll welcome me right back into the fold. Don't you think?"

"Just don't use my name," he said, " 'cause that would be spooky."

"Oh, I won't."

Longarm had a strong urge to kiss this woman but he resisted. "Virginia, you go back to Iowa and become a lady. And while you're on the train, you'll have plenty of time on the eastbound to create lots of details, which everyone back there will certainly expect. Can you do that?"

"I can," she told him. "I'll weave a story about our love that will wring their hearts and fill their eyes with salty tears."

"Don't overdo it," Longarm advised. "Don't get carried away with the story."

"I won't. But I'll act like I'm heartbroken and deep in mourning. I'll even wear black for a few weeks. I'll rub charcoal under my eyes so they'll think I can't sleep for the grieving of my husband's passin' and rub onions in my eyes so it looks like I cry every minute that I'm alone."

"Are you sure that isn't overdoing it a bit?"

"Naw! The bachelors in my hometown will fall all over themselves to comfort me. Besides, Marshal, I look really good in black. It makes my blond hair stand out golden."

"Yes, I can well imagine that."

"You're a handsome man, Marshal Long. I could be talked into staying here with you in Cheyenne for quite a spell."

"I'll take that as a compliment."

Her lips formed a small pout. "But I suppose that Miss Danner has already got her meat hooks in your hide."

"Nope."

"Well, you could do a lot worse than her," Ginny said. "She's a pretty woman and has a lot of money, I'll bet."

"I think that she does. But I'm not interested in money."

"That's because you've never been a dirt-poor homesteader. Money isn't everything but it sure would be nice to have some for a change."

"Maybe you'll marry a wealthy man back in Iowa," he suggested.

"I don't know about that but I damn sure won't marry another poor one and I won't go back to any farm."

Longarm almost smiled knowing that this woman would do just fine. "Good-bye and good luck, Miss Macklin."

"Same to you, Marshal. And if Fagan has family out in Montana half as mean and dangerous as he was, you're going to need plenty of luck. Take care of that bad shoulder."

"I will."

Longarm left the woman in room #8 and hurried off to catch his train. He tried not to think of what Fagan must have done to her back at the Knott homestead. But what he admired about Virginia was that she had moved past that and was already scheming to present herself in a whole new and sympathetic light when she returned to her childhood home. And, maybe it was wrong to think this way, but he hoped that Miss Virginia Ann Macklin's abusive father had already up and died.

Chapter 16

His trip to Helena took two weeks and was uneventful and tedious. Longarm arrived by stagecoach with an aching but nearly mended right shoulder. He had been in Helena a few years earlier and knew that the town had succeeded the gold camps of Bannack and Virginia City to become Montana's territorial capital in 1875, only eleven years after gold had been discovered. The gold hadn't lasted very long but the town was advantageously situated near plenty of water, timber and some of the best grazing in the West. The summers were short but pleasant, and the snow came early and stayed late. In Montana, the winters were much harder than in Denver and it was not uncommon for especially bad ones to bring huge die-offs among the area's vast cattle herds.

All that considered, Helena was a beautiful city and Longarm could see that it had grown only a little since his last visit. As soon as he climbed down from the stagecoach, he headed for the local marshal's office not wishing to get off on the wrong foot as he had done back in Cheyenne.

The marshal of Helena was named Jimmy Roscoe and he was about six feet tall with black wavy hair and a quick smile that flashed a perfect set of teeth. When Longarm introduced himself, Roscoe extended his hand, which was soft but had power in the grip. Despite the man's easy smile, Longarm had the feeling Roscoe was tough to the bone. He was in his early thirties and his heavily muscled arms and shoulders warned even a casual observer not to take the marshal of Helena lightly.

"So what brings you to our territorial capitol on this fine summer afternoon?" Roscoe asked, indicating that Longarm should take a seat. "Care for a cigar?"

"Thank you," Longarm said, noticing that Roscoe's cigar looked to be of far higher quality than the ones he smoked. "Don't mind if I do."

"I order them from New York City," Roscoe told him. "They're expensive but a lawman has to have a few luxuries in life. Ain't that right?"

Longarm judged that the man's boots, now resting on his desk, must have cost fifty dollars at least. "I couldn't agree more," he said, lighting the cigar and thinking it was one of the finest he'd ever had the pleasure of smoking. "These from Cuba?"

"That's right. Havana, to be exact. I'd like to go there someday. I hear their dark-skinned women are tall and passionate. Be fun to drink rum and smoke Cuban cigars. Might be a good place to consider retiring. You know, a man gets tired of cold winters and they don't get much colder than they do here in Montana."

"I expect that's true," Longarm said, deciding that Jimmy Roscoe must have inherited some real money to be thinking of retiring in Cuba and buying these quality cigars.

"So how was your trip from Denver?"

"Eventful."

"You're favoring your right arm," Roscoe said. "You have some kind of accident?"

"I was shot in the shoulder while on the train between Denver and Cheyenne."

"Shot on the train? My oh my. Did you kill the man that did it to you?"

"Not at the time," Longarm said. "But I punched his ticket a few weeks later in Cheyenne."

"Good," Marshal Roscoe said, blowing a smoke ring overhead. "I killed my last man just three nights ago in the Red Dog Saloon."

"What'd he do to you?"

"The cowboy was drunk and insulting. Called me a dude and a dandy."

"And you shot him for that?"

"Naw! I pasted the barrel of my gun over his head, but I was mad and hit him a little harder than I'd intended. He musta had a soft skull because it cracked and he died a couple of days later."

Longarm was appalled but tried not to show it. "So what did the judge say?"

"He said that cowboy had been drunk too often and he insulted everyone when he was in that state. The judge fined me ten dollars and ordered me to give the fine to the mortician to help pay for the casket."

"I see."

Roscoe winked and chuckled. "But I *kept* the money. They buried that dumb, egg-headed, trash-talkin' cowboy in an Indian squaw's dirty old blanket!"

Longarm didn't think that was a bit funny and concentrated on his cigar, which was easy enough to do.

"So, Marshal Long, what brings you to Helena?"

Longarm saw no point in beating around the bush. "Well," he began. "I was walking down Colfax Ave, which is right near my Denver federal office, last month when two men murdered a pedestrian in broad daylight."

"And what has this to do with Montana?"

"It turns out that all three . . . the murderers and the victim . . . were from Helena."

Roscoe's gray eyes widened slightly. "And their names were?"

"The victim's name was Chester King. I'm sure you know him and his family quite well."

Roscoe groaned. "Sonofabitch! So someone killed poor Chester."

"I'm afraid so. Just like they probably did in his older brother."

Roscoe's eyes narrowed. "How would know about that?"

"Chester didn't die right away," Longarm said, not wanting to offer any more information than was necessary.

"Who killed him?"

"One of the men was never identified," Longarm replied, studying the local lawman closely. "But the other one . . . who gave me this shoulder wound on the train, was named Fagan."

"Fagan?"

"That's right. Tell me about him."

Roscoe pursed his lips and shook his head. "I've never heard of anyone named Fagan."

Longarm's jaw almost dropped. "He and the other man were both big with black hair and coarse features. They were ruthless killers after some imagined treasure they believed was hidden or buried on Jed King's ranch."

Roscoe shrugged his thick shoulders. "I'm afraid you have me over a barrel on this one, Marshal Long. Jed King's ranch is going on the auction block for unpaid taxes in two weeks."

"Is that a fact?"

"It is," Roscoe said. "And I don't mind telling you that the judge along with several other friends intend to buy it."

"Why?"

"Why not? Anything wrong with a man investing in a profitable ranch partnership?"

"Not at all," Longarm said. "So what happened to Dave King and his sister?"

Roscoe looked him right in the eye and replied, "I'll be damned if I know. They're probably going to leave this part of the country. They've had a real run of bad luck the last year or two."

"Yeah," Longarm said, "sounds like. By the way, have you been the marshal of Helena for very long?"

"Nope."

"Where did you come from?"

"Texas and other places."

Longarm had a strong sense that this man was either an outright liar or else he was just holding back a lot of information. In his pocket, Longarm still had the telegram that he'd received in Denver saying that Jimmy Roscoe refused to investigate the murders of Jed or Johnny King.

"By the way," Longarm said, "did you know that Jed King was a United States Marshal with a very illustrious career?"

"Nope. To me, he was just a cantankerous old man."

"Any idea who ambushed him this past April?"

Roscoe shook his head. "The old man was shot in the back with a big fifty-caliber buffalo rifle. Blew his heart right out the front of his chest. I went out there and poked around but there was nothing much to see except a lot of dried blood."

"Did you question anyone?"

Roscoe was beginning to fidget and get annoyed. "Who was I to question? Jed King might have been a big deal in your eyes, but around here he was a pain in the ass. Arrogant and not a bit friendly, so I hear. I expect the man had a lot of enemies, some gained while he was a federal law officer like yourself. Others after he bought his ranch and started grating on his neighbor's nerves along with everyone else in Helena."

"Then you're telling me that you have no suspects."

"That's right," Roscoe said. "You have a problem with that?"

"Only problem I have," Longarm replied, puffing on his Cuban cigar a little faster, "is that you don't seem one bit concerned about solving the murder."

Roscoe came to his feet and his eyes were blazing. "I think our conversation has come to an end."

Longarm wasn't quite ready for it to end and he didn't get out of his chair just yet. "What about Johnny King drowning in a river?"

"What about it?"

"That seems odd."

"Not to me it don't," Roscoe spat. "The river was spring fed by snow and high. Right now you'll see that it's bone dry. But Johnny got himself caught in a flash flood. It happens all the time."

"I think I'll go out and pay a visit to the ranch and talk to Dave and his sister."

"You just go ahead and do that, Long. And while you're out there, tell 'em both that they'd better be off the property one day after the tax auctioneer's gavel falls."

"I'll do that," Longarm told the man, knowing he'd far overstayed his welcome.

When he went outside, he was still smoking the expensive Cuban cigar, but its taste had soured. Longarm removed and tossed the cigar into the street, then ground it under his heel. Aware that he was being watched from the marshal's office, Longarm headed for the livery to rent a good saddle horse and then get directions to Jed King's cattle ranch.

Chapter 17

When Longarm got to the livery, he wasted no time in renting a good sorrel gelding along with a saddle and the other things he would need to move around this part of the country.

"That outfit will cost you two dollars a day or ten dollars a week," the old liveryman said. "Cash in advance and a thirty dollar deposit."

"Those are pretty stiff terms," Longarm told the man as he came up with the cash.

"That's a damned good horse, mister. He's only five years old and I broke him myself. He can outrun about any horse in town and he don't buck on cold mornings or quit on the hard trails. He don't stumble and he don't spook."

"Can you shoot a gun off of him?"

"Mister, you could shoot a cannon off his back and it wouldn't faze him in the least. That horse is worth a hundred dollars and he'd be worth even more except for one major shortcoming."

"What's that?"

"Red *hates* dogs. He goes after them every chance he gets and you can't do a thing to stop him. If he takes a bead on a slow or old dog, well, you might as well count that dog among the former living."

"Why does he hate them so bad?"

"When Red was a colt, a big dog caught him sleeping and bit him on the muzzle. Tore it up pretty good but I stitched it shut with hair from his own tail and he turned out just fine. But Red never forgt about that dog and he's on a crusade to kill every last one of 'em. I can't keep a dog here at the livery and I like dogs."

"That's interesting to know," Longarm said.

"You better remember it. You see a ranch dog come runnin' out barkin', you got to turn that horse away from the dog and set him at a gallop in the other direction. It's the only way to keep Red from the chase."

"Well, I don't expect to see dogs," Longarm said, giving the man his deposit and feeling lucky to have such a good mount.

The sorrel had three stockings and a blaze down its face. It had a deep chest and long legs that hinted at both speed and exceptional endurance. Longarm tied his belongings behind the saddle and mounted the gelding. "I need to go out to Jed King's ranch. Could you give me directions?"

"Head north about twelve miles then look east toward some big mountains. The ranch you're looking for sits right at their base. It's as nice a ranch as there is in these parts."

"Is it big?"

The liveryman shrugged his shoulders. "It ain't big but it ain't small, either. Maybe two thousand acres. Big enough to make a family a good livin'."

"But I hear it's on the auction block for back taxes. Would you know anything about that?"

"Nope. All I know is that the King family has had a passel of bad luck. Maybe Ruby and Dave just want to get out of this country before they get killed like Jed and Johnny."

"I see," Longarm answered, not seeing at all. "Did you know Jed King well?"

"Well enough." The liveryman toed the earth. "Jed wasn't a man that you'd spend time chewin' the fat with. He was all business but I found him to be honest. Old Jed would say what was on his mind and you could agree or disagree. He didn't care what anybody thought except himself. He was hard to work with but I'm told he was fair. His handshake was as good as his money."

"It's too bad he was ambushed," Longarm said.

"Yeah, it was a dirty damned shame."

"Do you have any idea—"

"No, I do not," the liveryman snapped, anticipating Longarm's question. "And now I better get back to my work. You treat that sorrel right, you hear. Red is my best horse and I'll be mighty unhappy if you run him too long and hard."

"I won't."

"And if he stomps somebody's dog to death, that's *your* problem, not mine."

"Fair enough. And you can rest your mind because I won't mistreat him," Longarm promised as he rode away wondering what he'd find and what he'd do when he got to Jed King's cattle ranch.

After all the time he'd spent riding trains and stagecoaches to get to Helena, the horseback ride north was pleasant and the gelding was a fast mover so Longarm made good time. He came to a barbed wire fence gate with a sign hanging on it that read NO TRESPASSING. Longarm didn't let the sign stop him. He dismounted, opened the gate and then closed it before remounting. Off in the distance to the east, right up against the mountains like he'd been told, sat a small ranch house and some out buildings.

The wind had picked up and there were huge and dark thunderheads moving in over the valley. Longarm tugged down the flat brim of his hat snug on his forehead and had the feeling that he'd be getting wet before he covered the last few miles up to the ranch house.

"Come on, Red, let's make some time and see if we can beat the storm."

The gelding was more than happy to run. It flattened its ears against its head and took off like a scalded cat. Longarm gripped his saddle horn, lowered his head against the heightening wind and raced up the road toward the ranch. The horse never slackened its pace as it ran hard up the grade past a herd of Longhorns and twenty or thirty exceptionally fine-looking saddle horses. Thunder boomed off the mountains and the stand of cottonwood trees that surrounded the cabin were being whipped into a frenzy. It started to rain.

The ranch house was modest and made of logs. It had a nice front porch and there was smoke peeling out of the chimney. A large, spotted dog climbed out from under the porch. Its ruff was up and it started to bark but Red took the bit in his mouth and went after it so fast the dog barely escaped back under the porch with its tail tucked between its legs. The gelding's ears were flat and it acted like it wanted to tear up the porch, but Longarm managed to get it under control.

142

"Dammit, Red, behave yourself!" Before Longarm could dismount, a young man and woman appeared with Winchesters cocked and pointed in his direction.

"Who are you and what do you want?" the man shouted into the deteriorating weather.

"I'm Deputy United States Marshal Custis Long from Denver! I came to tell you that your brother, Chester, was gunned down a few weeks ago."

The man was in his mid-twenties. He paled and the woman staggered and had to reach out and grab a porch post for support.

"Can I put Red up and come inside where it's dry?" Longarm shouted as a bolt of lightning struck a tree not fifty feet from the cabin. "It's getting nasty out here in this storm."

The brother and sister exchanged glances and both of them put their rifles down and came out into the rain to help. They were, Longarm thought, entirely too trusting. For all they knew, he could have been an assassin, one come to finish off the King family.

Once in the barn, the rain began to pound with great intensity. Longarm unsaddled the steaming sorrel and they showed him a stall to turn it into and then pitched it some good grass hay.

Longarm walked over to the barn door and stared out at the rain, which was turning to hailstones as large as banty chicken eggs.

"It's a real piss cutter, isn't it?" Longarm remarked, more to himself than to the brother and sister.

"Yep," the man replied. "So how did our brother die?"

Standing in the barn with the storm all around them, Longarm had to shout over the thunder but he gave them the sad details. Told them everything that had happened in Denver including how his boss, Marshal Billy Vail, had been beaten and almost tossed out of an upstairs office window.

"Billy killed one of them in his office and I gunned down the other one not long ago in Cheyenne. His name was Fagan and he tried to ambush me. He'd murdered another man, too. A homesteader named Everett Knott."

"Was it Fagan that put a bullet in your right shoulder?" Dave asked.

"Yes," Longarm said. "You're pretty observant. I didn't think I favored it anymore."

"You do," the young woman said. "I'm Ruby King and this is my brother Dave. I can't believe that Chester is dead."

"I'm sorry," Longarm told her.

The brother and sister exchanged glances and then Dave said, "Chester went to Denver to try and get a loan. He said he knew someone there and could get the money to pay our taxes. He was pretty much our last hope of saving this ranch."

Ruby roughly sleeved the tears from her face. "To hell with this ranch! It's brought us nothing but heartache! We'll let the bastards have it and get out of this country before they get us too."

"Who are *they*?" Longarm asked. "Who is behind all this?"

"Marshal Jimmy Roscoe. Judge Wilbur." Dave shrugged looking bitter and defeated. "Who knows who else?"

"Who was the other man besides Fagan that came to Denver?"

"I'd bet anything he was Hank Fagan," Ruby said. "You killed Ace Fagan. They were tough men and friends of both the judge and the new town marshal."

Longarm studied Ruby for a moment as the rain cascaded down just inches from their noses. She was a tall young woman, probably five-foot-ten and willowy with sad brown eyes and long auburn colored hair. Her face was dark from too much sun and she had thin, chapped lips but fine, high cheekbones. Ruby King was no beauty queen but she was appealing and could probably hold her own with any cowboy on a roundup.

Her brother, Dave, was about the same height but stocky and square jawed. He had gotten his nose broken more than once and it was crooked but he would still be considered ruggedly handsome by most women. He had Ruby's brown eyes but his hair was more reddish and, despite looking dejected by the news of Chester's death, he looked tough.

"Let's make a run for the cabin," Ruby suggested. "We could stand here in the barn for hours. I've got a fire going and some hot coffee. But after hearing about Chester, I think Dave and I could use a few shots of brandy."

"Did my brother die in a lot of pain?" Dave asked just before he sprinted for the cabin.

"No," Longarm lied. "He went fast."

Ruby took off running across the ranch yard, her boots splashing in the mud. Longarm and Dave were right behind and when they made the porch, they removed their boots, hats and coats and left them outside.

"Have a seat, Marshal Long," Dave said, going to add some logs to the fire because the temperature was turning cold.

Longarm didn't feel like sitting so he went to stand near the fire. He let Dave and Ruby go off for a few minutes to grieve alone and his clothes steamed by the big fire as it crackled and popped. When the pair returned about fifteen minutes later, Dave took a chair and indicated that Longarm should do the same.

"Why didn't you just send a telegraph to us about Chester being murdered in Denver?" he asked. "Why did you see fit to come all the way to Montana?"

"I did send a telegram," Longarm told them as he removed the crumpled message from his coat pocket and handed it to Jed King's youngest and last surviving son. "As you can see, it told me about your father being ambushed and about Johnny drowning in the river this past April."

"He never drowned!" Ruby cried. "He was shot and dumped in the river."

"Can you prove that?" Longarm asked, thinking that he might have something to start with.

But Ruby shook her head and fought back tears. "No, by the time we found our brother's body . . ."

Ruby broke down and began to cry. Longarm could imagine what Johnny's water-swollen corpse must have looked like and it wouldn't have been pretty. A wide and swift river, even a narrow one, tore a body to shreds on submerged rocks and snags. Longarm had seen two men dragged out of fast rivers days after drowning and it wasn't something that he ever wanted to see again.

"I need a drink instead of hot coffee," Dave said, getting up and marching over to a cupboard where he found a bottle. "Ruby?"

"Two fingers at least in my coffee cup. What about you, Marshal Long?"

"I'll have the same."

They sat by the fire in silence at first, all of them just listening to the thunder and thinking about the loss of

Chester and the other members of what was left of the King family.

"So why did you come?" Ruby asked.

"Your father was a legend to me and my boss. We wanted to do whatever it took to get to the bottom of why he and your brother died."

"It ain't hard to figure," Dave told him. "They were murdered."

Longarm knew that but there was another question that needed to be answered. "Did your father have gold or money hidden on this ranch?"

They looked at him as if he were daft. "Now why would you ask such a question as that?" Ruby asked. "If we knew about any hidden money, do you think we'd let this ranch go to the auction block?"

"No, I don't," Longarm replied. "But there are rumors that he kept some of the money he'd recovered from hold-ups over the years."

Dave was on his feet, face crimson with anger. "Are you saying my father was a damned thief? Is that what you're trying to say?"

"Sit down and take it easy," Longarm told the young hothead. "I'm not accusing your father of anything. I just said that there is a rumor money is buried somewhere on this ranch and that could be part of the reason why you can't pay your taxes."

Ruby set her coffee cup down on the stone hearth. "Marshal, I don't get your drift."

"All right," Longarm said, "let me explain. How much do you and Dave know about paying taxes on this ranch?"

They looked to each other and Dave turned to say, "We never paid taxes. Pa handled the money and the bills."

"Then anyone," Longarm continued, "could say you

owe back taxes and you wouldn't really know if that was true . . . or not."

"I . . . I suppose that's true," Dave said. "But we got a bill from the tax man saying we owe twelve hundred dollars. You want to see it?"

"Yes," Longarm told him.

A few minutes later, Dave returned with the overdue tax bill which, in Longarm's opinion, looked legitimate. At the bottom was the signature of a man named Amos Reed. "Do you know Mr. Reed?"

"Sure," Ruby said. "He's been the tax collector for years."

"Who does he work for?"

Ruby took a sip of her hot coffee laced with brandy. "Why, he works at the territorial courthouse."

"And that," Longarm said, "would be under Judge Wilbur, would it not?"

"It would indeed," Dave said, a glint of understanding coming into his eyes.

Longarm studied the fire a moment to give himself and the pair a little time to think. Finally, he said, "I'll go back to Helena and have a talk with Mr. Reed and his boss, Judge Wilbur."

"You can't go out in this storm," Ruby told him. "And the day is almost done. Stay here for the night and go back tomorrow."

A cannon-shot of lightning hit somewhere close and Longarm thought that was a dandy idea but courtesy demanded him to say, "You've just had some very bad news and I don't want to impose."

"You're not going to impose," Dave said. "We had about resigned ourselves to the fact that something had happened to Chester. He should have returned weeks ago. We had a bad feeling about it."

"We're strong people," Ruby said. "Father taught us that much."

"Are there any more Fagan brothers that I should know about in these parts?" Longarm asked.

Dave emptied his glass of brandy and reached for the bottle. "As a matter of fact there are," he said. "Two to be exact."

"And are they cut from the same bloody mold as Ace and Hank?"

The siblings exchanged a quick look and then Ruby said, "I hate to tell you this, Marshal Long, but the two that are still alive are the worst of the whole, murdering bunch."

"Well isn't that just great," Longarm muttered with exasperation as he went over to get some more brandy and learn whatever else he was going to be up against here in Montana.

Chapter 18

When Longarm walked into the territorial courthouse in Helena, he asked to see the tax collector, Amos Reed. He was directed to a small and extremely cluttered back room filled with file cabinets and boxes stuffed with papers.

"Mr. Amos Reed?" Longarm asked the bespectacled little man hunched over his desk reading documents.

"Yes?" Reed answered, barely raising his head. "Who are you?"

Longarm introduced himself as a federal marshal and got right to the point. "I'm here to find out how much back taxes are owed by the King family on their ranch north of town."

Reed removed his spectacles and squinted at the big federal marshal. "They owe exactly twelve hundred and six dollars."

Longarm raised his eyebrows in question. "Mr. Reed, how many tax accounts do you handle in this county?"

Reed was caught off guard by the question. "I . . . I don't understand what that has to do with anything."

"How many?" Longarm repeated, his voice taking on an impatient edge.

"About six hundred or so."

"What I want to know, Mr. Reed, is how you remember the exact amount overdue in taxes on the King family's ranch, but you're not even sure of the exact number of accounts in this county."

Reed began to squirm. "Marshal, I don't see the relevancy of that question and I want to know what right you have in demanding information from me."

Longarm pulled up a chair without being invited to do so. "So how is it you know the exact amount of back taxes owned by the King family?"

"I . . . I was just working on that account."

"I don't believe that, Mr. Reed."

His face flamed with color and he tried to muster up some indignation, but it quickly wilted under Longarm's steely glaze.

"Mr. Reed, I want to see the account files on that ranch."

"The what?"

"I want to see the King family ranch account and I want to see it for the last five years."

Sweat actually began to bead on the tax collector's forehead. He drew out a rumpled handkerchief and mopped his face. "I . . . I can't do that."

"Why not?"

"The records are missing."

Longarm shook his head. "I think that they're missing because you *want* them to be missing."

Reed's lower lip began to quiver and his voice became shrill. "Marshal, how dare you insinuate that I am involved in any wrongdoing!"

Longarm banged his fist on the little man's desk so hard that a lead paperweight jumped into the air and fell to the floor. "I *demand* to see what written information you have on the King Ranch account."

"I . . . I refuse."

Longarm grabbed the man's ear and twisted it hard. "Show me!"

Reed squealed like a pig but he nodded his chins and found the documents that were resting on his cluttered desk. "Here," he blurted. "This shows the letter that I sent to the ranch and the amount of back taxes."

"You could have fabricated this amount."

Reed squirmed. "Please let go of me!"

Longarm snatched up the papers and studied them closely. They indicated that no taxes had been paid on the ranch in over three years.

"Judge!" Reed cried, his face bent close to his desk and turned to the open door. "Judge Wilbur, help me!"

Wilbur appeared a moment later and he was a big man gone to seed, probably in his late fifties. "What is going on here?" he demanded in a deep, rumbling voice.

Longarm introduced himself and explained the purpose of his visit. He ended by saying, "I want proof that the King family owes this office twelve hundred dollars in back taxes."

"Proof?" the judge thundered. "How dare you come into my courthouse, insult and assault my employee and then have the audacity to demand information that is none of your concern."

"I'm making it my concern, Judge. And, if you won't cooperate, I'll immediately go to the territorial governor and demand an investigation into what I believe is an outright land grab."

"Get out of here!" Wilbur bellowed. "Get out before I have you arrested and thrown in jail."

"On what charges?" Longarm asked.

"On the charge of trespassing on government property and attacking a government official!"

Longarm glared at the judge. "I am convinced that you, Marshal Roscoe and several others . . . including this little tax clerk . . . are in cahoots in order to gain control of the King Ranch. And I mean to prove it."

The judge yelled, "You have one minute to leave this courthouse or I will have you arrested and jailed!"

Longarm knew that he could not risk going to jail so he left, but not before saying, "I'm going to get to the bottom of this deception and then I will arrest everyone responsible including you and Marshal Roscoe."

"Get out of here and never come back!" Judge Wilbur bellowed.

Longarm was livid as he stormed out of the courthouse building. He went directly to the governor's office, but the man had left for Washington, D.C., and would be gone for three weeks. It was the worst sort of timing for, by then, the King Ranch would be sold at auction for back taxes and the game would be lost.

What am I to do? Longarm wondered as he stood on the corner of the street and tried his best to figure out a way to help Dave and Ruby avoid a tax foreclosure.

He went to the telegraph office and shot off a long telegram to Billy Vail explaining the circumstances and asking for advice.

"Send it immediately," Longarm told the operator. "I'll be back in an hour to see if I get a reply."

"Yes sir," the telegraph operator said. "But I should

warn you that an answer isn't likely to come back that quick."

"If Mr. Vail gets the message, it will."

Longarm had some time to kill so he went to a saloon to sip a beer and have something to eat. It wasn't much of a saloon and he didn't even note its name as he entered the dim interior and walked across the sawdust floor to the bar.

"I'm thirsty for a beer and a sandwich."

"Our specialty is pickled eggs and hogs feet."

"No thanks. I want a sandwich."

"We make a good beef sandwich on rye bread with fried potatoes on the side. Cost you six bits. Be an even dollar with the beer."

"Sounds good."

Longarm took his beer and went to a table to wait for his sandwich. He didn't notice the two large men that followed him inside the saloon and then ordered a couple of drinks. Their backs were to him and they fit in with the half dozen other customers that were present. The talk was low and Longarm was so preoccupied with his troubles that he didn't even notice when the two big men took a table in the dimmest recesses of the saloon near the rear entrance.

When his sandwich arrived, Longarm paid the bartender. He was ravenous and watching the bar when one of the big men stood up and walked out the back door. A moment later, his companion drew his gun and took aim at Longarm.

The beer glass in Longarm's fist exploded. Shards of glass cut his face as his eyes were momentarily blinded with beer foam. Longarm dove for the floor as another shot exploded in the saloon and rolled under his overturned table. He used his right hand to draw his gun and two more slugs came his way. With sawdust in his nostrils, he fired three times fast and saw the man that had tried to kill him stagger out the back door.

Longarm jumped up wiping blood, sawdust and beer from his face. He ran to the back door and saw the man he had wounded trying to escape down the alley. Longarm yelled, "Stop or I'll shoot!"

The big man did stop but he had no intention of surrendering. Instead, he fired again and Longarm drilled him in the chest. At the same time, the one who had left earlier jumped out from behind a rain barrel.

Longarm felt a bullet whip-crack past his cheek as he pivoted on his heel and used his last three bullets to drop the man.

The alley was filled with gun smoke. A feral cat screeched and ran zigzagging down the alley. Dogs began to bark and then, perhaps catching the scent of death rising from the alley, to howl.

Longarm went over to the fallen men and realized that he'd just had the very good fortune to kill the last two remaining Fagan brothers. Their resemblance to Ace and Hank was unmistakable.

Longarm turned around and reentered the saloon. He hadn't finished his beef sandwich and ordered a replacement along with a fresh beer.

The bartender's hand shook as he poured Longarm a beer and he said, "Did you kill them both?"

"Yep," Longarm said.

The bartender's hand shook even more and he used a dirty rag to wipe the bar top clean. "Those were the Fagan brothers. There's two more of 'em that will be coming after you for sure."

"Are you referring to Ace and Hank?"

His eyes widened in surprise. "Why, yes I am."

"Then there's nothing for me to worry about, mister." Longarm took a long pull on his beer. "Would you please get started on another beef sandwich? I never got to finish the first one, but what I ate of it tasted damned good."

"My gawd," the bartender whispered. "Don't you understand? You've just killed two men and made yourself a mortal enemy of their brothers."

"The Fagan brothers are *all* dead now," Longarm said loud enough for every man in the room to hear. "And I'm still waiting for that second beef sandwich."

"Oh my good gawd!" the bartender swore as he hurried to make another sandwich.

Chapter 19

Longarm was just finishing his sandwich and preparing to return to the telegraph office when Marshal Jimmy Roscoe and a deputy burst into the saloon. Roscoe was furious and his deputy kept his right hand on the butt of his gun, which made Longarm plenty nervous.

"What the hell," Roscoe cried, "are you doing in my town?"

Longarm drained the last of his second beer and slowly turned to the corrupt marshal. "Are you referring to the two Fagan brothers that tried to kill me . . . or to that little tax cheat, Amos Reed?"

"Both!"

Longarm studied the marshal for a moment then turned to his deputy and said, "If you don't get your hand off that gun, I'm going to take it away from you and jam it down your throat . . . sideways."

The deputy swallowed hard and moved his hand away from his gun. Longarm turned his attention back to Roscoe. "It was self-defense in here and in the alley. There are people here who saw the whole thing and will back me up on that."

Roscoe whipped his head around and stared at the customers lined up along the bar. "Did anyone see the shooting?"

They all nodded and one of them said, "That man is telling the truth. He was sitting over there at the table eating a sandwich when the Fagan brothers tried to gun him down."

That wasn't what Marshal Roscoe wanted to hear. "All right," he hissed, "you're a federal marshal and you haven't been in my town but a couple of days and you've already killed two men and left the courthouse in an uproar."

"That's because your judge and his tax clerk are in cahoots to defraud the King family out of their ranch. And you know what, Marshal Roscoe, I'm pretty sure that you're in on their crooked game."

Roscoe rocked back on his heels and threw a punch. Longarm had expected it. He ducked and drove a short, powerful left uppercut into Roscoe's belly that lifted the man completely off the sawdust floor. Roscoe tried to recover, but Longarm smashed downward with his elbow catching the lawman in the nose and breaking it with a loud crack.

Roscoe's deputy started to make his play but Longarm spun the nearly unconscious marshal around and shoved him hard. Roscoe crashed into his deputy and both of them went down. By then, Longarm's gun was in his hand and pointing at the two men.

"Don't you ever try to brace me again," he warned. "The thing I hate most is a crooked lawman."

Roscoe was cradling his bloody nose in his hands and

the deputy was scooting backward through the sawdust toward the door. Longarm walked past the deputy and outside wondering if Billy Vail had returned his message by telegram.

"No sir," the operator said when Longarm returned. "No message from Denver yet."

"Billy might be in a meeting," Longarm mused aloud. "When the message comes, hang on to it until I return. And don't even think about giving it to Roscoe or his deputy."

"But . . . I'd have to if I was under their orders."

Longarm knew that was the truth and that there was no point in pushing the issue so he said, "Just try to keep it to yourself. I'm a United States Marshal and there are going to be some changes made in Helena. I hope you like your job and want to keep it."

"Oh, I do! I have a big family and need this job, Marshal Long."

"Then find a way to keep my messages private," Longarm warned as he left the office.

He went out and mounted Red. Minutes later, he was galloping north again, determined to sort things out with Dave and Ruby.

The way that Longarm saw it, there wasn't any way of proving that Jed King had or had not paid his taxes unless they could come up with receipts filed away at the ranch. Other than that, the only thing that could be done to change the course of events unfolding in Helena was to come up with the twelve hundred dollars.

Maybe, Longarm thought, there *is* money hidden on the ranch. Money that could be used to pay the taxes and end this mess until he could figure a way to bring down the corrupt territorial officials.

Failing that, Longarm was afraid that even he could not save the King Ranch.

When Longarm arrived back at the ranch house, the sun was low on the horizon and the sky was starting to turn pink and salmon colored with a beautiful Montana sunset. Longarm went through the gate and again noted the Longhorn cattle scattered and grazing across the hills. He stopped for a moment to admire the fine herd of horses and thought them as handsome a bunch as he'd seen in many years. Old Jed King must have been breeding a special line of horses because most of the ones that Longarm saw were blue roans, tall, long legged and deepchested animals that would catch any horseman's eye.

"They're almost as handsome as you, Red, but of another color."

When he arrived at the ranch house, Dave and Ruby were standing on the porch with coffee cups in their hands.

"Well," Ruby asked. "Did you find out anything in town?"

"I sure did," Longarm told them. "I found out what I'd already suspected and that's that the town is a nest of thieves."

"Beginning with the marshal," Dave said.

"No," Longarm corrected, "beginning with Judge Wilbur. I did manage, however, to eliminate two of 'em."

"What do you mean?" Dave asked.

"I sent a telegram to my boss, Marshal Billy Vail in Denver, asking for his suggestions when I was nearly shot."

"In the saloon?"

"That's right." Longarm then told the brother and sister

162

about the last two Fagan brothers opening up on him and how he'd managed to put them down for keeps.

"Holy cow!" Ruby said. "You are either very good or very lucky."

"A little of both, perhaps."

"What about Marshal Roscoe?"

"He was madder than a teased snake," Longarm assured them. "He and Judge Wilbur are in this together. Do either of you have any receipts for tax payments your father made during the last few years?"

They shook their heads and it was Ruby who toed the ground a moment before saying, "The sad truth of the matter is that our father did everything with a handshake. Bought his horses and cattle that way and sold them the same way. If a man asked Father for a Bill of Sale he'd give them one, but it was just a hen's scratch that didn't mean much. Father was literate, but he hated to write anything and that included his name."

"There's something else we need to tell you," Dave said.

Longarm dismounted. "I'm listening."

"Father once mentioned that he wasn't getting tax bills. He chuckled about that and figured it was an oversight that could go on for years. So maybe . . . probably . . . we do owe a heap of taxes on this ranch."

"It wasn't an oversight," Longarm said. "It was deliberate. My guess is that the judge and his friends knew the way your father thought and took advantage of it. That's why you're about to lose this ranch unless we can come up with the cash."

"We don't have any cash."

Longarm ran his fingers through Red's mane as he tried to phrase his next words properly. "I have to ask you this again . . . are you sure that your father didn't have some cash squirreled away? You know, maybe something for a rainy day. Never mind how he got the cash, I'm just asking you because we have to think of something."

The brother and sister exchanged glances. "Well," Dave finally said, "Pa didn't trust the bank in town. I know he kept a small amount of ready cash there, but he never trusted them."

"Then maybe he did hide money here on the ranch."

"But wouldn't he have told us about it?" Ruby asked.

Longarm shook his head. "Not necessarily. Or, he might have been planning to tell you but never quite got around to it. Are there any hiding places that you can think of off the top of your heads?"

"Our father spent a lot of time in his barns," Ruby said. "I suppose he might have kept a hidden cache of money in one or the other of them."

"Then that's where we ought to start looking," Longarm said.

Dave looked doubtful. "I think it's a real long shot."

"Any better ideas on how we can raise the money?"

"No," Dave said.

"Then I suggest the three of us really search the barns carefully. Do some digging and prying and pulling of boards. Look everywhere."

"All right," Ruby agreed. "I think it's worth a try."

"Good," Longarm said. "I'll feed Red and we'll get started."

"Anything else happen in Helena?" Dave asked.

Longarm frowned. "Well, as a matter of fact I did have a run-in with Roscoe and his deputy. I had to hit your marshal a couple of times and I broke his nose. The deputy didn't want any part of it so he didn't get hurt."

"Oh no," Ruby moaned. "Jimmy Roscoe is as vain as a peacock! He'll never forgive you for marring his face."

Longarm threw up his hands. "Well, that's a cryin' shame but it isn't going to cause me to lose any sleep."

Ruby had to smile. "Marshal Long, all I have to say is that I'm really glad you're on *our* side."

Chapter 20

The ranch had three barns. The largest was used to store winter grass hay in a loft. Below the loft were a half dozen stalls for horses, newborn foals and calves, sick animals that needed protection from the elements, grain bins and piles of fresh straw. The second barn housed a hay wagon, two buckboards, a dozen ranch saddles, leather working materials and all kinds of harness and tack in various states of repair. The last barn was a carpentry and blacksmithing shop with a forge, anvil, shovels, pitchforks and about every other tool or implement that a ranch needed to operate year-round.

"Let's each take a barn," Longarm suggested after breakfast early the next morning. "I'll start with the one full of wagons and saddles. Dave, why don't you take the hay barn and Ruby can search the workshop."

"Sounds good," Dave said.

"If we don't come up with anything, we can switch around so that each barn will get three inspections," Longarm said.

"Where do we look and how?" Ruby asked.

Longarm frowned. "I'll search all the boxes and sacks as well as cracks where money could be stuffed. We could spend months digging up the dirt floors but we don't have that kind of time. Still, you should lift up or shift barrels and boxes just in case your father buried the money under them."

"Those are big barns," Ruby said. "This is going to take some time."

"What else do we have to do?" Longarm said.

"We could also check the house."

"That's true," Longarm agreed. "But it isn't very large so that won't take much time."

Longarm went into the barn and quickly searched the buckboards and hay wagon. Next he went to every saddle that had a saddlebag attached to it and inspected those to see if they were being used as a hiding place for cash. No luck. Finally, he moved some boxes and barrels around and examined the ground underneath them to see if the earth was soft and showed any signs of having been disturbed.

Nothing.

He examined all the walls for hiding places and studied the rafters and ceiling but thought it unlikely they were used as a hiding place. After an hour, he went to the hay barn and helped Dave finish his search.

"Not a thing," Dave said, looking discouraged.

"Let's go see if your sister has had any better luck."

Ruby King was on her hands and knees going through boxes of old harness. It was dusty, dirty work but she was taking her time and being thorough. Longarm crouched beside her. "Did you look through all those boxes of tools?"

"Not yet."

"Dave, we can go through those."

Most of the tools were broken. Old shovel heads, hammer heads, busted pieces of metal and used horseshoes. It was clear to Longarm that the ex-marshal Jed King had been a man who hated to throw anything away.

"Now here's something," Dave said, holding up a cracked pair of old saddlebags that had been buried in a tool barrel full of broken and rusting haying parts.

Longarm smiled. "There's not a reason in the world that something leather should be in a barrel full of rusty metal. Open the bags, Dave."

Dave opened them and slipped his hands inside. "My oh my!" he whispered, "I think I feel money!"

He pulled out stacks of greenbacks and Longarm could see that they were all large denominations. "Looks like we struck pay dirt," he told them.

"Hurry," Ruby said, "and count it."

"Can you imagine this," Dave crowed. "Our father coming out here to hide all this cash!"

Longarm drew a cheroot from his coat pocket and struck a match. He inhaled and leaned against a post as the two surviving members of the King family counted the cash.

"There's $890 here!" Ruby said. "Nearly nine hundred."

"Then we're about three hundred short of paying off the taxes," Longarm said. "Let's keep looking just in case your father had a few more places where he hid cash. And we've still got the house to search."

They spent four more hours looking high and low for money but never found any. By then, it was the middle of the afternoon and they were pretty sure that $890 was all that was going to be found.

Longarm walked around the ranch yard. "Your father might have hidden some in coffee or bean cans and buried them out here," he said, "but that seems doubtful. Have you got anything we can sell for three hundred quick dollars?"

The brother and sister thought about it. Dave said, "We could sell the buckboards and hay wagon but I doubt we could get that much for them. And besides, we need those wagons to operate."

"What about all those old saddles?" Longarm asked.

"Naw," Ruby said. "The whole bunch of them wouldn't bring a hundred dollars."

"Then you need to sell some horses or cattle," Longarm told the pair. "They're a quick sale and those horses look especially valuable to me."

"They were Pa's pride and joy," Dave said. "I sure wouldn't want to sell his horses."

"They're not his horses anymore. They're your horses," Longarm reminded him. "And what good are the horses if you lose the ranch?"

"Good point," Ruby agreed. "Dave, remember that Colonel Tyler over at the fort wanted to buy some of our horses and said he'd give us fifty dollars each for them? That's about double what he said he'd pay for most saddle horses used by his cavalry soldiers."

"Yeah," I remember. "But that was this spring. He may have changed his mind."

Longarm felt he had to jump in on this one. "Sure he may have, Dave. But then again, he may not have. I just don't see any choice but for us to drive about half of your blue roan horses over to the fort and see if you can get

170

enough money to pay off the taxes and then to pay next year's as well. That way, you're in the clear for a while and have some breathing room."

"I agree," Ruby said. "We have no choice."

"And there's one other thing," Longarm said, his expression grim. "I know that the Fagan brothers killed Chester in Denver, but I'd like to find out who ambushed your father this spring and who also killed your older brother, Johnny."

They nodded in agreement. "It might have been the Fagan brothers," Ruby said. "They were certainly capable of murder."

"That's right," Dave said, "but Jimmy Roscoe might have also been in on it. He's a dangerous man."

"They think that your father has a fortune buried on this ranch," Longarm said. "And whether that is true or not doesn't really matter. All we can do is to make sure that they can't get their hands on it."

"But what about Judge Wilbur?" Ruby asked. "I think that, sooner or later, he'll figure a way to take this ranch."

Longarm had given that matter some thought. "I have friends in high places," he said. "As a federal officer, I can ask that there be a review of the judge and his verdicts and background. It could be that Judge Wilbur has a few skeletons in his closet. If that's the case, he can easily be persuaded to disappear or else face the consequences of his past actions."

"Isn't that reaching for something that probably won't happen?" Dave asked.

"Not necessarily," Longarm assured him. "It's clear to me that Judge Wilbur has manipulated the tax man, Amos Reed. If he's done that in Helena, he's probably pulled some other shenanigans in other places. The next time I get to Helena, I'll make some inquiries. Send off a telegram or two and find out everything I can about your judge."

"But for now," Dave said, "we've still got to sell some horses in order to raise cash."

"That's about the size of it," Longarm agreed.

"We'll pick the ones we can bear to sell this afternoon," Ruby told them.

Longarm was pleased that they were going to take immediate action. "How far is the army fort that we have to go to sell the animals?"

"About a hundred miles," Ruby replied. "Two hard days or three easy ones. It's south of Helena."

"That's not good," Longarm said.

"Why?" Dave asked.

"Because it would be better if our enemies in Helena didn't know what we were up to. Is there some other way we can get to the fort?"

"Not unless we cross the mountains and that would add days to the journey," Ruby said.

"And," Dave added, "there's also the problem of leaving this ranch unprotected."

"Yes," Longarm said, "I hadn't thought about that, but you're right. If Marshal Roscoe learns that no one is here, he could burn the cabin and barns to the ground while we're gone and drive off or shoot the livestock that we leave behind."

"That would ruin us," Dave said. "I don't think we can take that risk."

"Then what would you suggest?" Longarm asked.

Dave expelled a deep breath. "Marshal, either you or me has to stay here. I don't see any way around it."

Longarm was afraid that he was right. And, while he

really wanted to be with these young people to protect them in case they were attacked while trailing their horses to the fort, he also knew that there was a very good chance that Roscoe and his friends would seize the opportunity to search for the treasure they were convinced had been hidden by old Jeb. And, when they failed to find it, they'd probably turn their rage into the act of destroying the ranch and stealing its valuable livestock.

"I'll stay," he said. "If they come looking for buried money and gold, I'd have the best chance of catching them in the act and killing them given that I'd have the element of surprise."

"We can go drive our herd of horses way out around Helena," Ruby said, looking determined.

"No," Longarm said. "If I'm going to set a trap here, I need them to think that your ranch is temporarily abandoned. That means that they have to be aware that you are driving horses to the fort."

"Marshal," Dave said, "what if they attack both us and the herd as well as come here to the ranch?"

"I don't think there are that many involved," Longarm said. "But, if I'm wrong, we could be outsmarting ourselves and cutting our own throats. However, I just don't see that we have any choice. Do you?"

They shook their heads.

"Then go select the horses you want to sell to the Army," Longarm said. "And plan to leave at first light in the morning."

"We'll be gone a week," Ruby told him. "And I pray that we don't come back and find that you've been . . . killed."

Longarm could see the deep worry in their eyes and he tried to make light of the situation. "You two are the ones that will be out on the trail driving horses and putting yourselves at risk of ambush. I'll be sitting here in your cabin eating and resting. I've got the easy end of this deal."

"Unless they all come here."

"I hope they do," Longarm said, meaning it. "Have you got some rifles in the house I can use?"

Ruby nodded. "Father had a real arsenal. We'll take plenty of firepower with us and we can shoot what we aim at so don't worry about us."

"My sister is right," Dave said. "Pa made sure that we became crack shots. And we'll leave three rifles and a double-barreled shotgun for you, Marshal Long. One of the rifles is a big old Sharps and it will shoot accurately up to five hundred yards; the other two are Winchester repeaters."

"Then I've nothing to worry about," Longarm said. "Your father built his house so that it commands the higher ground and it's surrounded by plenty of wide open grass. No one can sneak up on me here."

"Unless they come at night," Ruby told him. "But, if they do, our dog will hear them and start barking."

"That's right," Dave said. "Old Buddy will set up a howl that would raise the dead."

"He almost *was* dead," Longarm said with a smile, "when my horse spotted him coming out from under the porch."

Ruby and Dave must have seen Red go after their hound, Buddy. And while they also saw the humor there, they looked plenty grim as they saddled horses and went out to pick the horses they planned to drive a hundred miles to sell to the United States Army.

Chapter 21

Ruby and Dave left early the next morning driving ten of their father's prized blue roans. Longarm watched them go with a good deal of regret and apprehension. If he had guessed wrong, those two kids might be ambushed while he sat here at the ranch waiting for an attack that never happened.

"If you're attacked," Longarm had warned the pair just before they left with the sunrise bright in their faces, "take cover. If there are more than a couple pitted against you, let them have the herd. I promise that we can retrieve those horses later. The main thing is that you aren't killed."

Ruby had hugged Longarm and said, "Keep your eyes open and your powder dry. That's what our father always said. And, if you're surrounded and in deep trouble, you have that Red horse and a good chance of outrunning anyone."

"I'm not in the habit of running," Longarm had told her. "But there are times when one has to do it to fight another day."

So now the two young people that were all that remained of the King family were heading for some army fort a hundred miles away in order to pay the taxes and keep their beloved ranch.

"Godspeed," Longarm had said, waving as they disappeared over the horizon.

Now alone, Longarm felt a deepening sense of anxiety. Over and over that morning as he walked out to visit the remaining blue roans, Longarm kept asking himself if he'd made the right decision. He would never forgive himself if he'd sent Dave and Ruby on an errand ending in their deaths. And even if he did later manage to arrest or kill the murderers, it would be a hollow victory.

Longarm also thought about his boss, Billy Vail. No doubt there would be a telegram waiting in Helena from Billy probably offering money as well as encouragement and even federal assistance. Billy would be beside himself with worry but there was nothing that the man could do now. The trap was set and Longarm was sure that Jimmy Roscoe and friends would take this opportunity to make their move against this ranch headquarters.

He also knew that he would have a full day, perhaps even two before the ranch was attacked and their enemies tried to find what they thought was a hidden fortune. Given that much time, he decided to put it to good use and keep searching just in case there was some hidden loot buried around the yard or still in the barns that they had overlooked on their earlier searches.

Longarm found a shovel and went back to the barns. He had decided he would scrape and dig some shallow holes just to see if old Jeb King had buried the money where it was out of the weather and easy to reach.

He started digging in the hay barn because it was the

largest building and the ground there was soft with a two-inch cover of old hay, straw and horse manure. Longarm spent four hours poking and kicking and digging but came up with nothing.

"Are right, Jeb, I don't think you're the kind of man that would have put all his eggs . . . or money . . . in one basket. So we found a little bit of money now where would you have hidden the rest?"

Having satisfied himself that there was no buried treasure in the hay barn, he went next to the one that sheltered all the tools along with the anvil and forge. This, in Longarm's opinion, was probably where the ex-federal marshal would have spent most of his working time. He'd have been able to work in this barn during the wintertime because, in addition to the forge, it had an old barrel stove that would keep the barn tolerably warm. Longarm emptied the stove of ashes, thinking that maybe that's where he'd find a sack of money but all he got for his trouble were a pair of dirty hands.

Not in the least bit discouraged, he again examined all the barrels and boxes of discarded metal parts in the barn but came up empty. There was a rusted and broken-down old hay rake backed into a dim corner of the building that looked as if it were never going to be used again and Longarm wondered why Jeb had even bothered to keep it under cover. Maybe, he thought, the hay rake held the answer to more of Jeb's hidden cache of money. The rake had a big metal box attached with wire and it was crammed full of broken parts, mostly tines that turned the hay into windrows.

Longarm went through the box pitching out the busted parts even though he was sure that they had been removed in the earlier search by either Ruby or Dave. When the

177

box was empty, he bent to retrieve the parts and return them to the metal box. That was when Longarm noticed that the box had to have a false bottom because the rusty parts completely filled the box yet shouldn't have filled it but only halfway to the lid.

"Now why would an old metal parts box have a false bottom?" he asked himself out loud. "Unless it was a place to hide something *special?*"

Longarm eagerly hoisted the box and dumped its contents onto the dirt floor and then carried it seemingly empty out into the sunlight where he could have a much better look.

"Yep," he said, "it's a false bottom all right."

He used his pocket knife to jimmy the bottom up and then it lifted out easily to reveal stacks and stacks of cash.

"Eureka, I've found it!" Longarm cried, dropping to his knees and counting the money.

It took some time, but when he was finished, he had counted out a little over seven thousand dollars.

Longarm looked up at the sky and whispered, "Well, Jeb, did you steal this money over many years from the thieves you tracked down and killed? Or were you just a frugal man who saved most of his government salary not trusting the banks to keep it safe?"

Longarm doubted that there was any way the truth of how Jeb saved so much cash would ever be known. The bills he'd discovered were all used and most of them were of small denominations. There were no bill wrappers like one might have expected if the money had been taken from strongboxes or bank vaults. Instead, each pile of five hundred dollars was wrapped in string as neat as you please.

Longarm replaced five thousand dollars of the cash

back in the metal parts box and then re-covered it with the false bottom. He returned to the barn and refilled the top half of the box with the broken hay rake tines and rusty parts and set it exactly where it had rested on the old hay rake.

"I'll keep two thousand dollars for Dave and Ruby," he said to himself. "Sounds fair enough to me."

Longarm returned to the hay barn and stuffed the money under a pile of straw close to his saddle and bridle where it could be reached in a hurry. He pitched some fresh grass hay to Red and then curried the animal until its coat had a shine whistling a happy tune all the while.

"Red," he told the handsome gelding, "we might just have to make a run for it if too many come a'callin' tomorrow or the next day with murder and looting on their wicked minds. The man who owns you says you're as fast a horse as there is in this part of the country so we may just have to find that out."

Longarm had slept well that night and he didn't get up all that early. When he did rise, he went out to the barn, grained, watered and saddled Red. He led the tall gelding up close behind the house so it would be hidden from anyone coming up the road from Helena. Next, he went inside the ranch house and inspected the shotgun as well as the buffalo rifle and the two Winchesters. He also found a good Army Colt that had been converted to fire metallic cartridges.

"With all this firepower," he said to himself, "I will be able to hold off quite a crowd."

Longarm wanted the ranch to look deserted. He made sure that the dog stayed under the porch by tossing a ham bone way under the house. Then, he went back around to tighten his cinch and recheck the stack of money he'd taken.

It had occurred to him that, if he were killed by the marauders, he ought to try and leave some message for Dave and Ruby telling them where the five thousand dollars was hidden. On the other hand, if he were killed and left a message, it might be found by Roscoe or one of his friends. Maybe, he thought, I should put the whole seven thousand in my saddlebags and go after those kids heading for the army fort.

Longarm mulled the decision over all morning long and then he took a nap knowing that by now Roscoe and his friends would have received word that the King Ranch horses were being herded south and that the ranch would probably be temporarily deserted.

They should be here before dark, he thought. And then the fireworks will start and we'll have a death dance to see who ends up still standing.

Chapter 22

Marshal Jimmy Roscoe, his deputy and three other raiders came galloping boldly up the road from Helena just after midnight. Longarm was dozing by the front door with the big Sharps buffalo hunting rifle resting at his side. Marshal Roscoe and his men didn't expect there to be anyone at the ranch waiting for them, but they were cautious nonetheless.

"Spread out, men!" Roscoe called when they were yet a mile from the log cabin and ranch buildings. "We'll sweep in from the left and the right just in case there's someone waiting in ambush."

Longarm heard the dog growl under the porch. The dog had finished off the ham bone and was now standing in the yard, ruff up and fangs bared. It began to bark and Longarm knew it was scared because of so many fast approaching horses, galloping up the road in the dark.

The riders separated and there wasn't enough moon or starlight to tell which one was Jimmy Roscoe so Longarm eased out on the porch and let the dog bark as he placed the Winchesters close at hand near the chairs. He hoisted the heavy Sharps knowing that he would be invisible to the approaching riders as long as he stayed in the deep shadows on the front porch.

"Well, Marshal Roscoe, I'd sure like to know which man you are and put this first .50 caliber bullet through your chest. Maybe you're the one just slightly in the lead, about four hundred yards out. I ought to be able to punch your ticket to hell if this rifle shoots as accurately as promised."

Along the front porch was a rail made of old peeled pine and upon this rail Longarm rested the heavy buffalo rifle. He took careful aim and squeezed the trigger aiming just high enough to miss the horse's bobbing head but with every intent of striking the largest part of the rider's broad chest.

The Sharps boomed and Longarm saw fire spout from its barrel. His target jumped completely out of his saddle as if plucked by an invisible wire. Longarm saw the man do a somersault over the rump of his racing horse, strike the ground and bounce like a ball.

As soon as he'd fired the big rifle, Longarm snatched up a Winchester as the riders peeled off. He opened fire knowing they were still a bit out of range but hoping to get lucky.

And he did. One of the riders lurched sideways clinging to his saddle horn and then toppled to the ground, rolling to a dead standstill.

"Two down and three to go," Longarm said as the riders jumped from their horses and sprinted for what little cover they could find on the open, grassy slope.

Longarm concentrated on one particularly large silhouette and sent a hail of rapid-fire bullets in the man's direction. He was rewarded with a cry and then the attacker disappeared against the dark grass.

"Three down and two to go," he said, emptying that rifle and reaching for the second Winchester.

But the other two men had vanished, probably lying flat and crawling toward the ranch buildings.

Longarm grinned wolfishly. The odds were only two against one now and that suited him just fine.

A bullet came ripping toward the ranch house and it splintered the porch. Some of the splinters must have struck the barking dog because it yelped in pain and flew back under the porch. Longarm gathered his Winchesters and ducked back inside. He slammed the front door shut and hurried through the house. There was a back door that opened from the kitchen and he used it to slip outside into the darkness.

"Easy, Red," he crooned, calming the nervous gelding. "This will be over pretty quick and I intend to be the last man standing."

The horse quieted and Longarm eased around the side of the porch with a rifle in one hand and his six-gun in the other. He studied the yard for several minutes straining to see or hear one of his last two enemies. But having lost three members of their party already, they were being very cautious.

Longarm wondered if they would be foolish enough to try and rush the house or if they'd wait as long as it took before he was sighted. It was his experience that men like these were apt to lose patience and make a fatal move.

"Sit still and wait for them to come to you," he whispered to himself.

The dog under the porch was whining and Longarm

wondered if it had actually been shot. The sound of the dog caused Red's ears to flatten and he stomped his feet wanting to root out the cur and finish him off.

"Easy," Longarm hissed in a barely audible voice. "That dog isn't going to be any trouble to you."

The silence of the night stretched on. One hour, then two then three and four. Longarm had misjudged and underestimated this last pair. They were patient and smart. He wondered if they were waiting for daylight in the hopes that it would give them the killer's advantage.

He tried to remain absolutely still and in hiding but the gelding was getting more and more upset by the constant whining of the dog. Longarm knew that the two remaining attackers could hear Red and would be wondering why there was a horse tied behind the ranch house.

Out in the yard with dawn breaking to the east a rooster began to crow.

The night air was chill and Longarm wished he had his coat. The dog and horse kept up their nonsense and the rooster crowed even louder as sunrise flooded across the ranch yard revealing details in especially sharp focus.

They're as cold as I am and they'll be coming soon, Longarm thought. It must be near freezing. Maybe I should go inside and get my coat before I'm too numb to react quickly. I could put my freezing hands in the pockets to keep them warm enough to work a trigger.

Longarm decided that was a good idea. He slipped back into the kitchen and found a coat. The interior of the house was still very dark. He also traded the Winchester for the double-barreled shotgun before he eased back outside to stand by the corner of the house near the gelding.

Suddenly, he saw a bright light arc through the growing sunrise and it took him a moment to realize that one of the men had tossed a torch into the hay barn.

They expect that to draw me out, but it won't.

Longarm hated like hell to see the largest barn catch fire. It didn't take but a few minutes until the thing was roaring with flames.

Dave and Ruby will have to replace that barn but they can do it for only a few hundred dollars while they have thousands coming from the hidden cash I found . . .

It was fortunate that there were no animals in the hay barn, but Longarm's consternation grew when the second barn was also torched. He swore in anger thinking about the hay wagon, the two buckboards, the ranch saddles and tack that were all being lost. But there was nothing he could do about it. The two burning barns were standing apart in the open and the only way he could get to them was to cross the ranch yard and expose himself to a cross fire.

Damn their hides, anyway! Why did they have to set fire to perfectly good barns? I'll bet that . . .

It hit him like a thunderbolt. They would burn the third and last barn down next and it was the one that had the five thousand dollars hidden in the metal box attached to the old hay rake. The rake would survive but the cash would become ashes!

Longarm was furious. He knew that he wasn't going to be able to stay hidden while the last barn containing all that money went up in flames.

No damned way could he let that happen!

Longarm holstered his six-gun, untied Red and climbed into the saddle. He cocked back both hammers of the shot-gun and hissed at the stomping gelding, "Let's see how fast you *really* are."

He tied the reins in a knot near the saddle horn, reined

the gelding around back of the house and booted it hard in the ribs. Red shot out across the yard and Longarm let it run for all it was worth. Halfway across the yard, he saw a man jump out from behind a water trough and raise his gun. Longarm swung the shotgun in the man's direction and fired with both barrels.

The man crashed over into the water trough, almost torn in half. Longarm pitched the shotgun away and drew his six-gun. The gelding shied from the flames and veered hard to the right almost spilling Longarm who then reached down and reined it toward the third barn containing the hay rake and cash.

Jimmy Roscoe had been hiding behind a broken-down wagon and now he jumped out and opened fire. Longarm felt a bullet pluck at his coat and then he was booting Red into the last barn. The animal was running so hard it skidded across the barn floor almost impaling itself on the hay rake. Longarm leapt from the saddle and rolled on the barn floor.

Shots came searching into the dim interior as Roscoe stood in the open doorway firing fast. Longarm slid to a stop, raised his gun and smiled because the marshal of Helena was framed in the bright morning sunlight.

He fired twice and each bullet scored a lethal hit. Roscoe kept backing up and Longarm emptied his gun into the man making every bullet count.

"Five killers down and none to go," he said as he stood up and went over to Red who was shaking with fear. "Easy boy, this party is over."

He remounted the horse and rode out into the yard and the pasture noting the dead men and surprised to see that one of them, the first one he'd shot, was Judge Wilbur.

"No fool like an old fool," Longarm muttered, thinking

how once the fires were out, he'd have to find a shovel and start digging graves. He hoped that the ground was as soft as it looked from horseback.

By the time that Dave and Ruby King returned, what was left of their two ignited barns were just piles of warm ashes. Longarm saw their immediate and shocked reaction when they realized their great losses.

"At least you saved the *one* barn," Ruby told Longarm. "But I don't know how we're ever going to find the money to replace the other two."

"I do," Longarm said, handing the pair a huge bundle of cash.

"What . . . where . . . how did you get all this!" Dave blurted in astonishment.

"Found it in the last barn that I managed to save or they'd have also burnt it trying to flush me out."

"How much is it?" Ruby asked, eyes glued to the cash.

"A bit over five thousand. Plenty enough to hire men to rebuild the barns, pay your taxes for ten years or so and do whatever else you need done on this place."

Their eyes widened with wonder and Longarm invited them into their own house. They'd want to know who was buried under the freshly mounded graves. They'd want to know how he had managed to kill five men, including the town's corrupt judge and marshal.

Longarm wasn't sure exactly how he'd explain it. He was just lucky when it came to guns and bullets.

Lucky and pretty damn fast.

Watch for

LONGARM IN THE TALL TIMBER

309th novel in the exciting LONGARM
series from Jove

Coming in August!